Clunk-clunk-clunk.

Startled by the sound, Carrie gripped the steering wheel of her car even more tightly as she drove through the rain. The car suddenly veered left, crossed the center line and crashed into the ditch that edged the roadway.

Rain pelted the windshield. She struggled to free herself and clawed at the door, unable to push it open.

"Help!" she cried, knowing no one would hear her.

"Carrie!"

Tyler! He grabbed the door handle and ripped it open. Reaching around her, he unbuckled her seat belt. "Are you all right?"

She nodded. He pulled her free.

Rain pummeled her face as she looked into eyes filled with concern.

She swallowed down the fear and nodded. "I...I'm okay. How—"

He turned to study her car, then glanced back to where the wheel lay on the edge of the roadway. Retrieving the tire, he pried off the hubcap. "Three of your lug nuts are missing."

Her ears roared, and she shivered in the chilly rain.

"Someone tampered with your wheel, Carrie," he said, his voice deathly calm. "They wanted the tire to fall off."

Debby Giusti is an award-winning Christian author who met and married her military husband at Fort Knox, Kentucky. Together they traveled the world, raised three wonderful children and have now settled in Atlanta, Georgia, where Debby spins tales of mystery and suspense that touch the heart and soul. Visit Debby online at debbygiusti.com, blog with her at seekerville.blogspot.com and craftieladiesofromance.blogspot.com, and email her at debby@debbygiusti.com.

Books by Debby Giusti

Love Inspired Suspense

Military Investigations

Magnolia Medical

Visit the Author Profile page at Harlequin.com for more titles.

PLAIN DANGER

DEBBY GIUSTI

HHARLEQUIN® LOVE INSPIRED® SUSPENSE

Recycling programs
for this product may
not exist in your area.

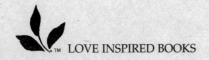 LOVE INSPIRED BOOKS

ISBN-13: 978-0-373-44721-3

Plain Danger

Copyright © 2016 by Deborah W. Giusti

www.Harlequin.com

Printed in U.S.A.

Store up treasure in heaven, where neither moth nor decay destroys, nor thieves break in and steal. For where your treasure is, there also will your heart be.
–Matthew 6:20-21

This story is dedicated to the wonderful readers
who buy my books and share them with their friends.
Your encouragement and support mean so much to me.
Thank you!

ONE

Bailey's plaintive howl snapped Carrie York awake with a start. The Irish setter had whined at the door earlier. After letting him out, she must have fallen back to sleep.

Raking her hand through her hair, Carrie rose from the guest room bed and peered out the window into the night. Streams of moonlight cascaded over the field behind her father's house and draped the freestanding kitchen house, barn and chicken coop in shadows. In the distance, she spotted the dog, seemingly agitated as he sniffed at something hidden in the tall grass.

"Hush," she moaned as his wail continued. The neighbors on each side of her father's property—one Amish, the other a military guy from nearby Fort Rickman—wouldn't appreciate having their slumber disturbed by a rambunctious pup who was too inquisitive for his own good.

Still groggy with sleep, she pulled on her clothes, stumbled into the kitchen and flicked on the overhead light. Her coat hung on a hook in the anteroom. Slipping it on, she opened the back door and stepped into the cold night.

"Bailey, come here, boy."

Black clouds rolled overhead, blocking the light from the moon. Narrowing her eyes, she squinted into the darkness and started off through the thick grass, following the sound of the dog's howls.

She'd have to hire someone to mow the field and care for the few head of cattle her dad raised, along with his chickens. Too much for one person to maintain, especially a woman who knew nothing about farming.

Again the dog's cry cut through the night.

Anxiety tingled her neck. "Come, boy. Now."

The dog sniffed at something that lay at his feet. A dead animal perhaps? Maybe a deer?

"Bailey, come."

The dog glanced at her, then turned back to the downed prey.

A stiff breeze blew across the field. She shivered and wrapped the coat tightly around her neck, feeling vulnerable and exposed, as if someone were watching… and waiting.

Letting out a deep breath to ease her anxiety, she slapped her leg and called to the dog, "Come, boy. We need to go inside."

Reluctantly, Bailey trotted back to where she stood.

"Good dog." She patted his head and scratched under his neck. Feeling his wet fur, she raised her hand and stared at the tacky substance that darkened her fingers.

She gasped. Even with the lack of adequate light, the stain looked like blood.

"Are you hurt?"

The dog barked twice.

Bending down, she wiped her hand on the dew-damp grass, then stepped closer to inspect the carcass of the fallen animal.

A gust of wind whipped through the clearing and tangled her hair across her eyes so she couldn't see. Using her unsoiled hand, she shoved the wayward strands back from her face, and holding her breath to ward off the cloying odor, she stared down at the pile of fabric that lay at Bailey's feet.

Her heart pounded in her chest. A deafening roar sounded in her ears. She whimpered, wanting to run. Instead she held her gaze.

Not a deer.

But a man.

She stepped closer, seeing combat boots and a digital-patterned uniform covering long legs and a muscular trunk.

Goose bumps pimpled her arms as she glanced higher. For half a heartbeat, her mind refused to accept what her eyes saw.

A scream caught in her throat. She turned away, unable to process the ghastly sight, and ran toward the house, needing the protection of four walls and locked doors.

The setter followed behind her, barking. Between his yelps, she heard a branch snap, then another. Straining, she recognized a different sound. Her chest tightened.

Footfalls.

Heart skittering in her chest, she increased her pace, all too aware that someone, other than Bailey, was running after her.

Coming closer.

She sprinted for the house and slipped on the slick grass as she rounded the corner. Catching herself, she climbed the kitchen steps and pushed open the door. Pulse pounding, gasping for air, she slammed it closed after Bailey scooted in behind her. Her hands shook as she fumbled with the lock. The dead bolt slipped into place.

She ran into the family room. Drawing the curtains with one hand, she grabbed the phone with the other and punched in 911.

Listening, she expected to hear footsteps on the porch and pounding at the door. The only sound was the phone ringing in her ear.

Grateful when the operator answered, she rattled off her father's address. "I found someone…in the back pasture. Military uniform. Looks like he's army."

Her father—a man she hadn't known about until the lawyer's phone call—had died ten days earlier. Now a body had appeared on his property. Touching the curtain that covered the window, she shivered. The horrific sight played through her mind.

"Someone c…cut the soldier's throat." She pulled in a breath. "So much blood. I…I heard footsteps, coming after me. I'm afraid—"

Her hand trembled as she drew the phone closer. "I'm afraid he's going to kill me."

Working late at his home computer, Criminal Investigation Division special agent Tyler Zimmerman heard sirens and peered out the window of his rental house. A stream of police sedans raced along Amish Road, heading in his direction.

For an instant, he was that ten-year-old boy covered in blood and screaming for his father to open his eyes. The memory burned like fire.

He swallowed hard and took in the present-day scene that contrasted sharply with the tranquility of the rural

Amish community where he had chosen to live specifically because of its peaceful setting.

Eleven years in the military, with the last six in the army's Criminal Investigation Division, had accustomed him to sirens and flashing lights at the crime scenes he investigated, but when the caravan of police cruisers turned into the driveway next door, Tyler's mouth soured as thoughts from his youth returned. Once again, violence was striking too close to home.

Leaving his computer, he hurried into the kitchen, grabbed his SIG Sauer and law enforcement identification before he shrugged into his CID windbreaker and stepped outside. The cool night air swirled around him. He hustled across the grassy knoll that separated his modest three-bedroom ranch with the historic home next door.

The flashing lights from the lineup of police cars bathed the stately Greek revival in an eerie strobe effect. The house, with its columned porch and pedimental gable, dated from before the Civil War when life wasn't filled with shrill sounds and pulsating light.

Men in blue swarmed the front lawn. Others hustled toward the field behind the main house. A woman stood on the porch, next to one of the classical white columns. Her arms hung limp at her sides. She was tall and slender with chestnut hair that swept over her shoulders and down her back. Her eyes—caught in the glare—were wide with worry as she stared at the chaos unfolding before her.

Gauging from the number of law enforcement officials who had responded, something significant had gone down. For a moment, Tyler switched out of cop mode and considered the plight of the stoic figure on the porch. Whatever had happened tonight would surely affect her life, and not for the better. Ty was all too aware that everything could change in the blink of an eye. Or the swerve of an oncoming car.

Approaching a tall officer in his midthirties who seemed in charge, Ty held up his identification. "Special Agent Tyler Zimmerman. I'm with the CID at Fort Rickman."

The guy stuck out his hand. "You've saved me a phone call to post. Name's Brian Phillips."

He pointed to a second man who approached. "This is Officer Steve Inman."

Tyler extended his hand and then pointed to his house. "I live next door and saw your lights. I wondered if you needed any assistance."

"Appreciate your willingness to get involved," Inman said with a nod.

"You probably know that the owner of the house, a retired sergeant major named Jeffrey Harris, died ten days ago," Ty volunteered.

"I remember when the call came in about his body being found." Phillips pursed his lips. "Seems he lost his footing on a hill at the rear of his property and fell to his death. Terrible shame. Now this."

Tyler pointed to the forlorn figure on the porch. "Who's the woman?"

"Carrie York. Evidently she's the estranged daughter of the deceased home owner." The taller cop glanced down at a notepad he held. "Ms. York called 911 at twelve-thirty a.m. She had arrived at her father's house approximately six hours earlier after traveling from her home in Washington, DC. She was asleep when her father's dog alerted her to the body. Supposedly the deceased is in uniform."

"Army?"

"Camo of some sort. Could be a hunter for all we know. Some of my men secured the crime scene. I'm headed there now. You're welcome to join me."

"Thanks for the offer."

Phillips turned to Inman. "Get Reynolds and question Ms. York. See what you can find out."

"Will do." Inman motioned to another officer and the twosome hustled toward the porch, climbed the steps and approached the woman. She acknowledged them with a nod and then glanced at Tyler as he fell in step with Phillips and passed in front of the house.

In the glare of the pulsing lights, she looked pale and drawn. A stiff breeze tugged at her hair. She turned her face into the wind while her gaze remained locked on Tyler.

Warmth stirred within him, and a tightness hitched his chest. The woman's hollow stare struck a chord deep within him. Maybe it was the resignation on her face. Or fatigue, mixed with a hint of fear. Death was never pretty. Especially for a newcomer far from home and surrounded by strangers.

He dipped his chin in acknowledgment before he and Phillips rounded the corner of the house and headed toward the field of tall grass that stretched before them.

"How well did you know your neighbor?" Phillips fixed his gaze on the crime scene ahead.

"Not well. I'm new to the area. We exchanged pleasantries a few times. The sergeant major seemed like a nice guy, quiet, stayed to himself."

Tyler had spent the last month and a half focused on his job, leaving his house early each morning and returning after dark. Being new to post and getting acclimated into his assignment didn't leave time for socializing with the neighbors.

The cop glanced left and pointed to the Amish farm house on the adjoining property. "What about the other neighbors?"

"Isaac Lapp's a farmer. He and his wife and their eight-year-old son are visiting relatives in Florida."

"Probably for the best, especially so for the boy's sake. No kid should witness a violent death."

Tyler's chest constricted. Without bidding, the memory returned. His father's lifeless body, the mangled car, the stench of gasoline and spilled blood. He blew out a stiff breath and worked his way back to the present. Why were the memories returning tonight?

Two officers had already cordoned off an area near the rear of the field and stood aside as Ty and Phillips approached. Ducking under the crime scene tape, they headed to where battery-operated lights illuminated the body. The victim lay on his side, his back to them. No mistaking the digital pattern of the Army Combat Uniform or the desert boots spattered with blood.

Grass had been trampled down as if there'd been a struggle. The earth was saturated with blood. The acrid smell of copper and the stench of death filled the night.

Ty circled the body until he could see the guy's face and the gaping wound to his neck. He paused for a long moment, taking in the ghastly sight of man's inhumanity. What kind of person would slice another man's throat?

The victim's hands were scraped. His left index finger was bare, but then not all married guys wore rings. Blood had pooled around his head.

Ty hunched down to get a closer view. *Fellows*, the military name tag read. The 101st Airborne patch on his right sleeve indicated he had served with the Screaming Eagles in combat. The rank of corporal was velcroed on his chest. The patch on his left arm identified that he was currently assigned to the engineer battalion at Fort Rickman.

"Looks like he's one of ours." Tyler stood and glanced at Phillips. "I'll contact the CID on post as well as his unit."

Pulling his business card from his pocket, Tyler handed it to the cop. "Let me know what your crime scene folks find. I'd like a moment with Ms. York as soon as Officers Inman and Reynolds end their questioning."

"No problem. Tell them you talked to me." Phillips pocketed the business card. "I'll keep you abreast of what we find."

Tyler retraced his steps to the house, climbed to the porch and tapped lightly on the door before he turned the knob and stepped inside. A young officer glanced at the identification he held up and motioned him forward.

Inman and Reynolds stood near the fireplace in the living room. Ms. York sat, arms crossed, in a high-back chair.

Inman excused himself and quickly walked to where Tyler waited in the foyer. "Was the victim military?"

Tyler nodded. "From Fort Rickman. I'll notify his unit." He handed the cop his business card. "The CID's resources are at your disposal. Let me know what you need."

"Glad we can work together." Glancing into the living room, Inman kept his voice low as he added, "I presume you want to talk to her."

"Whenever you're done. Has she provided anything of value thus far?"

"Only that she works as a speechwriter for a US senator in DC. Probably a big-city girl, with big-city ideas." Inman smirked. "She asked whether the FBI would be notified."

"And you told her—"

"That we'd handle the initial investigation."

Noting the agitation in the cop's voice, Tyler was grateful for the good relationship between the Freemont Police Department and the Fort Rickman CID, which hadn't always been the case from the stories he'd heard around the office. Things could change again, but currently the two law enforcement agencies worked well together. A plus for Tyler. Getting in at the onset of a case made his job easier and pointed to a faster resolution, especially on a death investigation.

"Maybe there's a reason she requested the feds," he suggested. "If she works for a senator, there might be something she's not telling you."

"Could be. We can check it out. She claims to have heard footsteps as she ran back to the house."

"Did she get a visual?"

"Unfortunately, no. She didn't see anyone. Could be an overanxious imagination, especially after finding the body. Still, you never know. People have been known to fake grief and shock."

"Did you get her boss's name?"

Inman glanced down at his open notebook. "It's here somewhere."

Tyler turned his gaze to the living area, feeling an emotional pull deep within him. Usually he didn't allow his feelings to come into play during an investigation. This case seemed different. Perhaps because her father had been a neighbor. The close proximity might have triggered a familiarity of sorts. Or maybe because she'd lost her father. Tyler could relate. Still, he hadn't expected the swell of empathy he felt for her.

"Here it is." Inman stepped closer and pointed to his notebook. "Ms. York works as a speechwriter for Senator Kingsley."

Any warmth Tyler had sensed disappeared, replaced with a chilling memory of a man from his past.

"Senator Drake Kingsley?" Ty asked.

Inman nodded. "That's right. You know the name?"

Worse than that, Tyler knew the man—a man he would never forget and never forgive. Drake Kingsley had killed his father, yet he'd never been charged for the crime.

TWO

Carrie's head throbbed and her mouth felt dry as cotton. Officer Reynolds appeared oblivious of her discomfort and continued to ask questions that seemed to have no bearing on the terrible crime that had happened tonight.

"Has Senator Kingsley had attacks against his person?" he asked. "Or have there been attacks on anyone with whom you work?"

"Not that I know of, but I don't see how what happens in Washington could have bearing on a soldier's murder in rural Georgia."

"Yes, ma'am, but I just want to cover every base."

"Bases as in baseball, Officer Reynolds, or the investigation?"

He looked peeved, which was exactly how she felt. Peeved and tired and more than a little frightened to think of what had occurred just outside her window while she slept. She'd never expected following the trail to her estranged father would hurl her into a murder investigation.

If she wasn't so confused, she would cry, but that wouldn't solve the problem at hand, namely to answer the officer's questions. Plus, she didn't want to appear weak. She'd been living alone long enough to know she had to rely on her own wherewithal. A lesson that had been one of the few good things she'd learned from her mother.

Not what she wanted to bring the memory of her deceased mother into the upheaval tonight.

"I'm sorry," Carrie said with a sigh. "My rudeness was uncalled for, to say the least."

"I know this must be hard for you, ma'am, but if you can endure a few more questions."

Which she did until her head felt as if it were ready to explode. She glanced at the leather-bound Bible on the side table, the stack of devotionals and religious texts on a nearby shelf and a plaque that read As for Me and My House, We Will Serve the Lord. All of which made her wonder if she had stumbled into the wrong house. How could she be so closely related to a man she didn't even know?

Exhausted and exasperated, she finally held up both hands as if in submission. "If you don't mind, I need a glass of water."

"Certainly. Why don't we take a break?" Officer Reynolds acted as if pausing had been his idea. "Officer Phillips will probably want to talk to you later."

She sighed. "I've told you everything I know."

"Yes, ma'am. I'll pass that on, but I'm fairly confident he'll have additional questions."

"Of course, he will." She stood, her gaze flicking to the man in the foyer wearing the navy jacket. He and Officer Inman were whispering as if they were talking about her.

Turning back to Reynolds, she asked, "May I bring you something? Water? Coffee?"

"No, thank you, ma'am. I'm fine." He closed his notebook and pointed to the door. "I'll step outside for a bit while you relax."

As if she could with so many police officers swarming over her father's property. Hurrying into the kitchen, she ran water in a tall glass and drank greedily, hoping to slake her thirst as well as the headache. She arched her shoulders to ease the tension climbing up her neck and glanced out the window at the neighboring brick ranch.

George Gates, her father's lawyer, had mentioned the army man who lived next door. She'd seen him come home earlier, when she fixed a cup of tea and nibbled on the chicken salad croissant the lawyer had been kind enough to have waiting in the fridge for her.

Tall and well built with short dark hair and a thick neck, the neighbor had US Army written all over him. Hard to mistake a guy who looked that all-American. She hadn't expected to see him walking across the front lawn earlier in his CID windbreaker. Now he was waiting for her in the foyer.

Did he even have jurisdiction this far from post? As much as she didn't want to answer any more questions, she didn't have a choice. Placing the glass on the counter with a sigh, she then returned to the living room.

Reynolds and Inman had left the house, leaving the younger cop guarding the door and the army guy standing in the entryway. She extended her hand and walked to meet him. "Carolyn York. My friends call me Carrie."

"Tyler Zimmerman. I'm a special agent with the Criminal Investigation Division at Fort Rickman. The CID is involved because the victim was military."

His handshake was firm and confident.

"Fort Rickman is where my father was last stationed,"

she stated in case he wasn't aware of her father's military past.

"Yes, ma'am. I understand you just arrived in Freemont."

She nodded. "A little before five and in time to talk to my father's lawyer briefly. Mr. Gates asked me to return to his office in the morning to discuss my father's estate, but—" She spread her hands and looked out the window. "I'm not sure if everything will settle down by then."

"I understand your concern, Ms. York."

She tried to smile. "Carrie, please. Since we're neighbors."

He quirked an eyebrow.

Had she revealed too much? "The lawyer mentioned that someone from the CID was my father's neighbor," she quickly explained. "I put two and two together. You do live next door?"

"That's correct." He motioned toward the living room. "Shall we sit down? I know you've answered a lot of questions already, but I'd like to hear your take on what happened."

She settled onto the couch while he pulled a straight-back chair close. Mr. Zimmerman seemed to be a man of few words with no interest in social niceties that could take the edge off the tension hovering in the air. She wouldn't make another mistake by trying to be neighborly.

As much as she struggled to remain stoic, a picture of what she'd seen played through her mind again.

The gaping wound, the bloody ground—

She dropped her head in her hands. "I'm sorry, but I...I can't get the image—"

"The man in the field?" the special agent filled in.

Pulling in a ragged breath, she glanced up and nodded. "The memory keeps flashing through my mind."

"Which is understandable." He hesitated a long moment, before asking, "What alerted you to go outside, ma'am?"

"It was Bailey." The dog lay by the chair where she had sat earlier. Hearing his name, he trotted to her side.

"I had let him out a little before midnight," she explained. "When he hadn't returned, I must have fallen back to sleep."

She rubbed the dog's neck, finding comfort in his nearness. "At some point, Bailey started barking. I went outside to get him, thinking he'd found an animal."

Mentally she retraced her steps, seeing again the mound that had turned into a man. "I never expected to find a dead body."

"Did you see anyone else or hear anything?"

"Footsteps behind me when I ran back to the house. I locked the door and called 911."

"After you made the call, did you hear or see anyone outside?"

"No, and I was too afraid to pull back the curtain. The only sounds were the sirens."

"Could you describe what you saw when you discovered the victim?"

"Blood, a military uniform, boots. At first, I thought he might have tripped and fallen. When I saw his face, I...I knew he...he was dead." Her hand touched her throat in the exact place the soldier's had been cut. "The wound was—"

She dropped her hand into her lap and worried her fingers. "I can't describe it."

"But you saw no one the entire time you were outside the house."

"That's correct."

"How did you learn of your father's death, Ms. York?"

"George Gates called five days ago with the news. That's when I learned Sergeant Major Harris was my father."

The agent glanced up from his notes. "Sorry?"

"I thought my father had died soon after I was born."

"Why did you think that?"

"My parents weren't married. My mother evidently fabricated a version of what had happened."

"She told you he had died?"

"That's correct. In a covert black ops mission."

The special agent narrowed his gaze. "And you believed her?"

Carrie bristled. "Don't children usually believe their mothers?"

A swath of color reddened his cheek as if he were embarrassed by his lack of sensitivity. "So you grew up not knowing Sergeant Major Harris was your father?"

"My mother told me my father's last name was Harrison, probably to keep me from learning the truth. I searched through military channels when I was in college, but the army disavowed having a record of a Jeffrey Harrison from Radcliff, Kentucky." She glanced up at the tall ceiling and crown molding, thinking of the lie her mother had perpetuated for too many years. Lowering her gaze, she focused on the photo of a muscular man in uniform. The name tag on his chest read Harris. "Now I find out my father lived in Georgia."

"What did your mother say after Mr. Gates notified you of the sergeant major's death?"

"My mother died three years ago of a heart attack."

"I'm sorry."

Carrie had grieved deeply for her mother, but she

wasn't sure how she felt now. After the phone call from Gates, she'd been numb and confused. Since then, the word betrayal had come to mind, although she knew her mother wasn't totally to blame for the disinformation she had passed on to Carrie. Surely the sergeant major bore some of the guilt, as well.

She hugged her arms, suddenly cold and overcome with fatigue. Once again, the line of questioning seemed to have digressed off track.

"Mr. Zimmerman," she said with a sigh. "I have no idea what is going on here. My father supposedly died from an accidental fall ten days ago. Finding another military man dead on his property tonight has me wondering if something suspect could be underfoot."

The agent leaned in closer. "Like what?"

She shrugged. "You tell me. Was my father involved in some nefarious or illegal operation?"

"Do you think he was?"

"I have no idea. According to his lawyer, Jeffrey Harris stipulated in his will that I was not to be notified of his death until after his burial. Mr. Gates presumed that my father didn't want me to feel coerced to attend his funeral. I must admit that I question my father's logic. It seems strange that he would be considerate of a daughter he'd never tried to contact."

Giving voice to what troubled her the most about her father brought even more unease to her already-troubled heart. Why hadn't her father wanted a relationship with his only child?

She glanced at the fireplace with its wide hearth and sturdy oak mantel and shook her head to ward off the hot tears that burned her eyes. She usually could control her emotions. Tonight was different. More than anything, she didn't want to seem needy in front of the agent with the penetrating eyes and questioning gaze. "I feel like I'm drowning, as you might imagine. No buoy or life preserver in sight."

"Ms. York…uh, Carrie, I'm sure things will sort themselves out over the next few days. How long do you plan to stay in Freemont?"

"I'm not sure. Mr. Gates mentioned that someone is interested in buying the property. He encouraged me to sell, and initially, I had planned to put the house on the market as soon as possible."

"And now?" the CID agent asked.

"Now I'm not sure."

"Then you plan to stay?"

"No." She didn't know what she planned to do. "I have a job in DC, but I can work here for a period of time. I'm sure the police won't want me to leave the area."

"Not until the investigation is over," he confirmed.

"Then that settles the problem. I'm forced to stay, although I'm concerned about safety issues with a man dead in the backyard. Still, I'll remain here, at least until the ceremony downtown."

"I'm unaware of any ceremony."

"Honoring veterans from the local area. Mr. Gates said a plaque with my father's name and years in service will be added to the War Memorial and unveiled at the end of the month. I'll stay until then."

"And if the investigation is still ongoing?"

Her shoulders slumped ever so slightly. "Eventually I'll have to return to my job."

"You work for Drake Kingsley?"

"That's right. I'm his speechwriter."

"Do you believe everything you write in his speeches?"

The personal nature of the question surprised her as much as the sudden hard edge to his voice.

Any residual tears instantly dried. "What does that mean?"

"He's not a friend of the military."

"Senator Kingsley is a good man." With a big heart, she almost added.

"If that's what you believe, then he's got you fooled."

The door opened, and Inman stepped into the foyer. "Officer Phillips needs to see you, sir."

The special agent pushed out of the chair and stood. "Excuse me, ma'am. I have work to do."

He turned on his heel and followed Inman outside, leaving her alone, except for Bailey and the young cop who stood guard at the door.

Recalling the special agent's curt tone and abrasive comment, she felt her heart pounding. The senator had been like a father to her over the past eighteen months that she'd worked for him. Demanding at times, but he was also generous with his praise, and her writing had improved under his tutelage.

Why would Special Agent Zimmerman be so antagonistic toward a noted public servant who played such an important role in her life? The senator had changed a few of her speeches over the months to tone down her exuberant support for the military. She had never purposefully maligned anyone in uniform, nor would she ever do so. The special agent didn't understand that she was a paid employee on Kingsley's staff and had to comply with his requests in regard to his talks.

Evidently Mr. Zimmerman was unaware of the number of people Carrie admired, all dedicated men and women who were serving in the military. She—and indeed, the entire nation—was indebted to their sacrifice.

Admittedly Senator Kingsley had been somewhat vocal in his disregard of those in uniform in private settings, and she had heard him say that the military wasn't to be trusted, but that was the senator's belief and not hers.

Unlike Kingsley, she was wholeheartedly pro-military.

Except she did wonder about the special agent neighbor. Not because he was in the army, but because he lived next to a murder scene and had so quickly appeared on site. Was it purely coincidental?

Carrie needed to be careful until she knew if the CID agent was trustworthy or someone to watch.

Tyler left the house and descended the porch steps to where Officer Phillips stood on the sidewalk, cell phone at his ear. Disconnecting, the cop acknowledged Tyler with a nod.

"The victim's wallet confirmed Fellows's name and provided an address." Phillips pointed into the wooded area behind the Harris home. "A dirt road winds along the rear of the property. The sergeant major kept a trailer in the woods and rented it out. Fellows was his latest tenant. Some of my guys are there now looking for anything that can shed light on his murder."

Tyler glanced back at the house. "I wonder if Ms. York was aware of the trailer. She plans to talk to her father's lawyer in the morning."

"George Gates?" Phillips asked.

"You know him?"

"I know of him," the cop acknowledged. "His office is just off the square. He's well thought of in town. Has a pretty wife, a couple kids. The wife is some kind of designer. Works with Realtors by staging the homes that are on the market. All high-end properties."

"Thanks for the information," Tyler said. "I'll pay him a visit in the morning."

"Doubt he'll provide anything new." Phillips smirked. "You know lawyers and client privilege."

"You're saying Harris had something to hide?"

"I'm saying you never know about neighbors." Phillips made a clucking sound as he stared into the wooded area before turning back to Tyler. "Did you ever see Fellows hovering around Harris's property?"

"Never. But then I've haven't been in Georgia long."

"Where were you stationed before Rickman?"

"Germany for three years. A little town called Vilseck."

"Near the Grafenwohr training area."

Surprised that Phillips knew of Grafenwohr, Tyler smiled. "You're prior military?"

"Roger that." The cop chuckled. "I enlisted after high school."

Tyler liked Phillips. Knowing he had served elevated him in Tyler's opinion even more. "Thanks for your service."

"My contribution was insignificant compared to most. Present company included."

Tyler appreciated the comment. At least Phillips would understand the role the CID could play in the investigation.

"With the army's concern about fraternization between the ranks, something seems strange to me," Phillips said as he pocketed his cell. "Why would a sergeant major rent his trailer to some young soldier?"

"Harris was retired, and even if he had been on active

duty, it wouldn't have been a problem if they were from different units. The sergeant major probably advertised on-post. Fellows may have been a country boy. Liked the outdoors and wanted to move out of the barracks."

The cop rubbed his jaw. "Maybe, although I wonder if anything else was afoot."

"I'll talk to his first sergeant and the other soldiers in his platoon," Tyler said. "They might provide a better picture of who Fellows was."

Phillips nodded. "And why someone wanted to kill him."

"What about questioning the neighbors?" Tyler asked.

"I've got a couple officers checking the folks who live nearby. I'm not sure how cooperative the Amish will be. They're good people, but they stick to themselves."

Tyler glanced at where the body was found. "The killer could have skirted Amish Road, by using the dirt road you mentioned. If he paid Fellows a late-night visit, they could have argued and gotten into a fight. Fellows might have run this direction to get away from the assailant. The killer follows and attacks after Fellows stumbled into the clearing."

"Did you hear anything unusual?"

Tyler shook his head. "Not a peep."

"Something must have alerted Ms. York."

"She said her father's dog found the body and started barking."

Phillips pursed his lips. "Might seem like a stretch, but I wonder if she could be involved."

Tyler hadn't expected the comment, but as any law enforcement officer knew, no one could be ruled out at this point.

The cop slapped Ty's shoulder. "My turn to talk to her."

Tyler pulled out his phone as the officer climbed the steps and opened the door. Carrie stood in the foyer and glanced around Phillips to where Tyler lingered at the bottom of the steps. She tilted her head ever so slightly as if questioning why he was still hanging around outside. The door closed, leaving Tyler with a strange sense of being shut out.

He had allowed his emotions to get the best of him when he questioned her. A mistake he shouldn't have made and wouldn't make again. Still, he hadn't expected an investigation in Georgia to open a painful memory from his past.

Pulling up his phone contacts, he tapped the number for the CID special agent on call. Everett Kohl's voice was heavy with sleep when he answered. "What's going on, Ty?"

"A soldier was murdered along Amish Road."

"Fill me in on the details."

Tyler shared what he knew about the case.

Once he had finished providing information, Everett asked, "Want me to notify the post duty officer? He'll inform General Cameron. The commanding general needs to know what happened."

"Sounds good. Thanks."

"Any witnesses?" Everett inquired.

"Not at this point. The sergeant major's daughter arrived in town late in the day. She knew nothing about her father until his lawyer called informing her of the property she had inherited."

"Welcome to Freemont."

"You've probably heard of Drake Kingsley, the senator from Ohio?" A ball of bile rose in Ty's throat. Not that he would share his past with Everett.

"As I recall, the senator's not enamored with the military."

"You're exactly right." Tyler paused for a moment before continuing. "Kingsley is talking about the need to slash the defense budget even more than last year. He was also instrumental in convincing the president to cut troop strength."

"What's the connection with this case?"

"Carolyn York, the woman who found the body, works as a speechwriter for Senator Kingsley."

Everett groaned. "She could be as vocal as her boss. We don't need any more bad press or do-gooders from Washington interfering with our investigation."

Tyler understood bad press. He also understood Everett's concern. Budget cuts and troop reduction had decimated the army. Combat readiness was a thing of the past.

"How'd you get involved, Ty?"

"I heard the sirens. Came to see what was going down and found out the deceased was military, assigned to the engineer battalion."

"That's interesting."

"In what way?" Tyler asked.

"Let me check the post paper. Seems I read the sergeant major's obit not long ago."

Tyler waited until Everett came back on the line.

"Here it is. 'Sergeant Major Jeffrey Harris, recently retired from the US Army.' This is the part that's of interest. 'His last duty station was Fort Rickman, where Harris was the command sergeant major of the engineer battalion.'"

"So he and Fellows could have served together, depending upon how long ago the corporal transferred to the battalion."

"Doubtful the sergeant major would rent a trailer to someone in the same unit, unless they had some prior connection." Everett voiced the same concern as Phillips had earlier. "Having a superior as a landlord could be seen as a conflict of interest."

"Something to consider."

Ty looked back at the Harris home. Carrie's arrival the night Fellows died could also be significant.

"This case could explode in our faces," Everett continued. "Especially since the woman has ties to Washington. I'll confirm with Wilson tomorrow to ensure that the boss is in agreement, but the way I see it, you'll need to keep tabs on Ms. York. Two folks have died on that property in less than two weeks. Keep her safe and as happy as can be expected under the circumstances. I'll let you know any information we find out about Fellows."

Everett was right. Tyler needed to keep an eye on his neighbor and see what he could learn about the estranged daughter and the young soldier who had died on her father's property. Maybe the pretty newcomer to Freemont knew more about her father than she was willing to admit.

THREE

The first light of dawn glowed on the horizon as the Freemont police climbed into their squad cars. Phillips stood next to Tyler, watching their departure.

"Our crime scene folks will expand their search over the entire field," Phillips said. "So far they haven't found anything that seems to have bearing. I'm hoping Forensics might provide more information. I'll let you know what we uncover."

"Earlier you mentioned that the sergeant major's body was discovered in the woods," Tyler said. "Do you know who found him?"

"Inman handled the call, but if my memory is correct, an Amish teenager took a shortcut through the property and stumbled across the remains."

"Was there anything suspect about Harris's death?"

Phillips shook his head. "Nothing that seemed questionable at the time."

"Might be worth reviewing the report," Tyler suggested.

"I'll do that. And I'll talk to Inman."

Tyler glanced at the lights glowing in the downstairs windows of the stately home. "Are any of your people still inside the house?"

"One of our rookies."

"I'll tell him you're wrapping up." Tyler hustled up the porch steps and rapped lightly on the door. The young cop he'd seen earlier answered his knock. Tyler stepped inside and repeated the message from Phillips. The officer hurriedly left the house and climbed into one of the squad cars.

Footsteps sounded from the kitchen.

"Ms. York?" Tyler called from the foyer.

She stepped into the hallway. Her eyes widened ever so slightly. "Agent Zimmerman, I didn't expect to see you again. Do you have more questions?"

"No, ma'am, but I wanted to apologize for my comments."

"Which comments are you referring to?" She squared her shoulders in a defensive gesture he had half expected after his earlier outburst.

"My comments about Senator Kingsley." Not that they weren't true. Still, he hated hearing the cool aloofness in her voice.

She stepped closer. "Evidently I said something wrong, something that upset you. Let me assure you that I'm not the senator."

He pointed a finger back at himself. "I in no way thought you were."

"Nor do I put words in his mouth."

"Actually…" Tyler hesitated. "If you write his speeches, that's exactly what you do."

She frowned.

He wasn't making points.

"Senator Kingsley is quite explicit on what he wants covered in each speech," she said with an icy stare. "His policies are exactly that—his policies. They reflect his opinions and what he believes to be true and do not reflect the way I think or feel."

"That's good to know."

"I admire all who defend our nation, Agent Zimmerman. They sacrifice greatly. Many give their lives for our security. I am indebted to their service, as the entire nation should be."

"Then we see eye-to-eye on that point, but I still hope you'll accept my apology."

"Of course."

He handed her his business card. "Some of the crime scene personnel will remain on-site for a while. I'm heading to post. My phone will be on if you think of anything else."

"I've told you everything."

"Yes, ma'am, but I'm sure you're anxious and concerned. Keep your doors and windows locked. Be alert to any danger."

Her stiffness crumbled. She drew her hand to her neck. "Y-you're worrying me."

Which he hadn't intended to do. "I just want to ensure that you use caution."

"Thank you for your concern."

When he'd entered the house the first time, his focus was on the murdered soldier and on finding information. Now that the immediate urgency was over, he paused to glance at the expansive living area with two brick fireplaces, tall ceilings and hand-hewn hardwood floors.

"Your home is beautiful."

"My father's home," she corrected. "I still feel like an outsider."

"In time, that should change."

Her face softened for a moment, exposing a vulnerability he hadn't expected. Then she pulled in a quick breath and returned to her former polite, but somewhat perturbed, self.

"I hope the investigation is wrapped up quickly, Agent Zimmerman."

"It will be." Tyler sounded more optimistic than he felt. "My cell's always on. You can call me if you hear anything worrisome. I'm home most nights by seven."

"Bailey's a good watchdog."

"I'm sure he is."

Tyler started for the door.

A phone rang. Carrie reached for her cell and checked the caller identification. "If you'll excuse me, it's the senator's office."

"You notified Washington?"

She quirked her brow. "Did you want me to keep the soldier's death secret?"

"Of course not." He opened the door. "I'll be in touch."

He hurried off the porch and started across the front lawn on his way home. Phillips waved from his sedan as he and Inman pulled onto Amish Road and headed back to town.

Tyler needed coffee and a shower before he drove to post, but he couldn't get past the churning in his gut, knowing Carrie York was on the phone to DC.

This case came with baggage. Not what he needed or wanted. He had to focus on the investigation instead of getting into a war of words with the senator's speechwriter whose arrival in Freemont felt suspect.

Was Carrie York an innocent bystander? Or was she somehow involved in the soldier's death?

* * *

After the congestion and traffic in DC, driving along the gentle, rolling hills and fertile farmland was a refreshing change of pace for Carrie. Some of the anxiety she'd felt through the night had ebbed by the time she arrived downtown.

She parked her car behind the lawyer's office and hurried inside. George Gates had been nice enough yesterday when he gave her the keys to her father's house as well as the information about Bailey and the kennel where the dog had been boarded. Everything had seemed like a dream, especially she realized the huge white home with Greek columns had belonged to her father.

Thankfully the dog's frisky playfulness and demand for attention had filled the expansive house with activity that added warmth and welcome to what could have been a difficult homecoming. She and Bailey had quickly become fast friends, and she was grateful for his attention. The pup had stayed close by her side, until he'd whined to go out shortly after midnight.

All too soon, the initial charm of the historic home had been marred by the discovery of Corporal Fellows's body. She hoped the lawyer would provide some clue to the soldier's death, which was the first question she asked George Gates once they'd exchanged pleasantries and she'd taken a seat in the chair across from his desk.

The lawyer was midforties, with whitened teeth, bushy eyebrows and a ruddy complexion that made her wonder if he frequented a tanning salon.

"I heard something had happened along Amish Road," he said, his voice somber. "Although I wasn't sure if the information I received was accurate. So you're saying a soldier was killed behind Jeff's house?"

"In the open field but close to the woods. As you can imagine, I'm upset and confused. Is there something you failed to tell me about my father?"

Surprise registered on his puffy face. "Surely you're not implying your father was involved in anything that would lead to a soldier's death."

"You tell me."

"Jeff was a good man, Carrie. He did a lot for Freemont and was well respected. The Harris family has been a part of this town's history since the early 1800s. Your father inherited the house and property from his maiden aunt some years back. He worked hard to restore the home to its former beauty, and since then, he's been a pillar of the town."

"Pillars can crumble."

He laughed off the comment. "I told you someone has expressed an interest in buying the property. It's something to consider. You're probably eager to return to Washington. I can handle the paperwork and expedite the sale."

She held up her hand. "It's too soon, George. I'm not ready to sell."

"You're upset, no doubt, about what happened last night. Take a few days to think it over. I'm sure the offer will please you."

"I came here today to find out more about my father's estate and especially his property. You didn't mention the trailer he rented."

"My mistake. You were tired yesterday. I hesitated taking up more of your time."

He taped a manila envelope on his desk. "A plat of the property is inside. Your father owned a hundred and twenty acres and the house. He rented out a trailer, usually to one of the soldiers from post. Almost half of his land is prime farmland. The rest is wooded."

"And you have an interested buyer for both the land and the house?"

"That's correct."

"Can you assure me the property won't be cut up for development?"

"I'm not sure what the buyer's plan would be, but it's nothing you need to concern yourself with at this point."

She leaned closer. "But it is my concern, George. I don't want to disrupt the beauty of the Amish community."

"Yes, of course. I understand."

Did he? Carrie wasn't sure about George Gates or his too-accommodating responses.

By the time she shook his hand in farewell, she had even more questions about her father, his past and her future.

Leaving the office, she hurried to her car and clicked the remote opener. Before she reached for the door handle, someone called her name. Turning, she spied Tyler Zimmerman climbing from a car parked on the opposite side of the lot.

In the light of day, he looked even taller and more muscular. Maybe it was the navy slacks and tweed sports coat he wore. For a moment she wondered why he wasn't in military uniform before recalling that CID agents wore civilian attire when working on a case. She'd stumbled upon the information while researching a speech for Senator Kingsley. Something about not wanting rank to interfere with their investigation.

"I didn't expect to see you here," she said in greeting.

He smiled as he neared. "I wanted to talk to Mr. Gates."

"You need a lawyer?"

His eyes twinkled, making him appear even more handsome.

"I want to talk to Mr. Gates about your father's rental property," he explained. "And see if he can provide information about your dad's relationship with Corporal Fellows."

When she didn't respond, he added, "I'm just gathering information, Ms. York."

"Carrie, please."

He smiled again.

Her heart skittered in her chest, making her feel like an adolescent schoolgirl. Too young and too foolish. Needing to shield herself from his charm, she clutched the manila envelope close as if it could offer protection.

He cocked his head. "What are you up to today?"

She tried to sound nonchalant. "In search of a grocery store."

"There's one on the way out of town. Turn left at Harvest Road. The supermarket's two blocks down on the left."

"Thanks." She opened her car door and slipped behind the wheel. "Good seeing you, Tyler."

Leaving the lot, she glanced back as the special agent opened the door to Gates Law Firm and stepped inside. Rounding the corner, she passed an Amish teenager who watched her turn right. Seeing the special agent had put her on edge. The pensive stare of the Amish boy added to her unease.

After a quick stop at the grocery store, she drove out of town, heading back to her father's house. Even the pretty countryside couldn't lessen her anxiety. In the distance, dark clouds filled the sky. Her heart felt as heavy as the thick cloud cover.

If only she could go back to the stories her mother had told her about the handsome army man who had swept her mother off her feet. They'd been young and in love and…well, things happened, including babies, or so she had explained when Carrie was old enough to learn the truth.

Only part of it had been a lie.

Her father hadn't died in a covert black ops mission as her mother had led her to believe. He wasn't part of the military's elite Delta Force, and the army hadn't covered up his death and withheld information from the grieving girlfriend who was pregnant with his child.

Now Carrie knew the truth, but counter to what scripture said, it hadn't set her free. Instead she felt tied in knots and suddenly connected to a man and a past she didn't understand, which only confirmed her upset with God. Why would He turn His back on a woman who always longed for a father's love? Evidently she and her problems didn't carry weight.

The special agent only confused her more. He'd been civil enough today, and his smile had seemed sincere, yet she had to be careful and cautious, especially after his antagonistic comments last night.

Carrie glanced again at the sky and turned on the windshield wipers as the first drops of rain began to fall. A road sign warned of a sharp curve ahead. She lifted her foot from the accelerator and placed both hands on the wheel as the car entered the turn.

A bolt of lightning cut through the dark clouds, followed by a clash of thunder that made her flinch. The tires lost traction for a heartbeat on the slick roadway.

She turned the wheel to the right and tapped the brake, relieved when the car responded.

Coming around the curve, she glanced ahead and gasped. A semi-trailer was bearing down on her, going much too fast. Heart in her throat, she intensified her hold on the steering wheel, feeling the pull as the truck flew past with less than an inch to spare.

Too close.

Clunk-clunk-clunk.

Startled by the sound, she gripped the wheel even more tightly. The car shimmied, then jolted as the rear left side dropped. She glanced back, seeing a tire roll across the roadway.

A grating sound. Metal dragging against pavement. Her heart raced. The car veered left, crossed the center line and crashed into the ditch that edged the roadway.

Rain pelted the windshield. She struggled to free herself and clawed at the door, unable to push it open.

"Help!" she cried, knowing no one would hear her.

"Carrie!"

She turned, seeing Tyler.

He grabbed the door handle and ripped it open. Reaching around her, he unbuckled her seat belt. "Are you all right?"

She nodded. He pulled her free.

Rain pummeled her face as she looked into eyes filled with concern.

"Where are you hurt?" He touched her arms, the back of her neck and head as if searching for an injury. "Talk to me."

She swallowed down the fear and nodded. "I…I'm okay. How—"

"I was driving home and saw your car enter the turn.

A semi passed. Then I saw you in the ditch. Did you get sideswiped?"

She shook her head. "The tire came off."

"What?"

He turned to study her car, then glanced back to where the wheel lay on the edge of the roadway. Retrieving the tire, he pried off the hubcap. "Three of your lug nuts are missing. Have you gone to a mechanic recently?"

"I had my oil changed before I made the trip to Georgia."

"This just happened. Since you last drove the car."

"I…I don't understand."

"In town. While you were talking to Gates. Someone removed three of your lug nuts."

Her ears roared, and she shivered in the chilly rain.

"Someone tampered with your wheel, Carrie," he repeated, his voice deathly calm. "They wanted the tire to fall off."

"But why?"

"Two reasons come to mind. Either to scare you—"

Her heart quickened.

"Or to do you harm."

FOUR

The police sedan's flashing lights drove home the seriousness of what had happened. Tyler glanced at his own car where Carrie sat, protected from the stiff breeze that had picked up once the rain eased.

"You must be working the twenty-four-hour shift," Ty said when Officer Steve Inman climbed from his patrol car.

Ignoring the dampness, the officer smiled. "You and Ms. York are keeping me busy."

Much to Tyler's frustration, Carrie left the warmth of his car and hurried to join them at the side of the road.

"Ma'am." Officer Inman nodded a greeting. "You mind telling me what happened?"

She quickly filled him in on losing control of the car and the missing lug nuts.

"Any chance your folks can dust the hubcap for prints?" Tyler asked. "You'll find mine, for sure, and the last mechanic who checked the tire."

"That won't be a problem." Inman pulled a notebook from his pocket. "So you think the lug nuts were purposely removed."

Tyler nodded. "I'm guessing when Ms. York was in town."

"I made two stops," she added. "The Gates Law Firm and the supermarket on Harvest Road."

Inman made note of the information. "I'll see if we have video cameras in either area that might have picked up activity."

"You'll let me know what you uncover," Carrie insisted.

"Yes, ma'am." He turned to Tyler. "You were following Ms. York home?"

"I had talked briefly with George Gates and ended up not too far behind her car, which was fortunate."

"Ma'am, did you see anyone behind you when you drove to town this morning?" the cop asked.

Carrie shook her head. "No one."

Inman turned to Tyler. "What about you, sir?"

"Negative. But I left my house early and went to post first so I could brief Chief Wilson, the head of the CID, on Corporal Fellows's murder. General Cameron has been informed, as well."

"He's the post commanding general?"

"That's right. As you can imagine, the general's upset about the corporal's death and has given us free rein to support you in any way we can."

"I'll pass that on. The chief of police is out of town, so Phillips is in charge. Last I heard, he contacted the Georgia Bureau of Investigation to rush the forensics on the case. Freemont is indebted to the military. We'll do everything we can to bring Corporal Fellows's killer to justice."

All of them turned at the sound of an approaching vehicle. Earl's Tow Service was painted on the side of the tow truck that pulled to a stop. A man hopped to the pavement.

"Craig Owens." The driver provided his name as he approached the threesome. "Special Agent Zimmerman?"

Tyler nodded. "That's right. I talked to Earl."

He pointed to Carrie's car, wedged in the ditch. "The vehicle needs to be towed. Earl said he'd order a new rear tire. Tell him to check the underbelly and ensure that nothing else is wrong."

"Will do." The driver held up a clipboard. "You mind signing the request for service?"

Tyler passed the clipboard to Carrie. "The car belongs to Ms. York."

"Do you need payment now?" she asked.

"No, ma'am, just your signature."

After she'd signed the form, the driver tossed the clipboard into his cab and climbed behind the wheel. He backed to the edge of the ditch and used a winch to hoist the vehicle onto the flatbed.

Once the car was safely locked down, he handed Carrie a business card. "Earl will call you with an estimate if your car needs repair work. As soon as the new tire comes in, he'll notify you. Appreciate your business."

Tyler stopped Owens before he climbed into his truck. "Any idea how long a wheel would stay attached with only two lug nuts?"

The tow man scratched his head. "Not long. The tire would start to shimmy and work the remaining lug nuts off in a short time."

Which was exactly what Tyler thought. "Thanks for getting here so quickly."

"We aim to please."

Inman slipped the notebook into his shirt pocket as the

tow truck headed back to town. "I'll let you folks know if we find any prints." He rolled the tire to his sedan and placed it in the trunk.

Then turning to Carrie, he added, "I might be jumping to the wrong conclusion, ma'am, but it looks like someone's not happy that you're in Freemont."

Tyler had to agree.

"Lock your doors and windows. Call my number or Special Agent Zimmerman if you feel threatened in any way or if anything else happens."

"Good advice," Tyler said to Carrie. "We're both worried about your safety."

"Use caution, ma'am," Owens continued. "As I said before, seems someone wants to do you harm."

Her face twisted with concern. "But why?"

The cop pursed his lips. "No clue, except it might tie in with the soldier's death."

"Or my father's," she added.

Tyler needed to learn more about the sergeant major. He wouldn't give voice to his suspicions, because it would upset Carrie even more, but just as she had mentioned earlier, her father could have been involved in something illegal that could play in to the corporal's death and have bearing on her accident today.

Inman nodded to Carrie and slapped Tyler's arm before he slid behind the wheel of his police sedan.

After ushering Carrie to his car, Tyler held the door for her as she settled onto the passenger seat. "I'm grateful Officer Inman responded to the call," he said as he climbed into the driver's side. "Someone without knowledge of what happened last night might not see the significance of the accident."

Her face was drawn and her eyes reflected both fatigue

and worry. "How would someone know where I was or which car in the lot was mine?"

"Your out-of-state tags would be easy to spot. Information travels fast in small towns. No telling who knew you planned to visit George Gates."

She shook her head. "But I didn't have an appointment."

"You told him yesterday that you would return in the morning."

"What if losing the tire was just a random act?"

Tyler sighed. "Having three lug nuts go missing is more than happenstance, Carrie."

"Then either someone's trying to scare me off, or it involves Corporal Fellows, as Officer Inman mentioned."

When Tyler failed to reply, she turned her gaze to the road. "Whatever the reason, the person responsible doesn't understand my determination to learn more about my father."

"Might be a good idea to program my cell number into your phone, Carrie."

"I already have."

They drove in silence until Tyler turned into the Harris driveway and parked at the side of the antebellum home. He glanced at the barn and the small chicken coop at the rear, seeing movement. His neck tingled a warning.

"Looks like someone's prowling around your property, Carrie. Stay here until I give you the all clear."

Before she could object, he slipped from the car and cautiously approached the barn, keeping his right hand close to the weapon on his hip. He stopped at the corner and watched as a man peered over the top of the coop.

"You're trespassing." Tyler raised his voice. "Put your hands in the air and turn around slowly."

The man complied without hesitation. Only he wasn't much over fifteen, with a shaggy haircut, suspenders and black pants. A hat lay on the ground, along with a bucket half filled with what looked like chicken feed.

"State your name and the reason you're on the Harris property."

"Eli Plank."

His clothing identified him as Amish. "Isaac Lapp asked me to feed the chickens while he and his family are out of town." The kid blinked. "I have done nothing wrong."

Tyler realized his mistake. "You can put your hands down, Eli. I didn't know anyone was helping out."

The boy lowered his arms. "Isaac has been caring for the chickens since Mr. Harris died. He asked me to lend a hand so he and his wife and Joseph could visit the boy's *Grossdaadi*. His grandfather."

"Where do you live?"

He pointed south. "The next farm. You know my *Datt*?"

Tyler shook his head. "I've seen him working in the fields, but we haven't met."

"Tyler?"

Hearing Carrie's voice, Tyler peered around the barn. She was walking toward them.

"Is everything okay?" she asked.

"Everything's fine." He introduced Carrie to the Amish boy and explained the reason Eli was on the property.

"Thank you for taking care of the chickens." Carrie opened her purse. "I'd like to pay you."

The boy shook his head. "I was helping Isaac. That needs no payment, but I must go home now." After returning the unused feed in the barn, Eli waved goodbye and hurried across the road.

"I don't think Eli is anyone to fear." Carrie watched as the boy approached the two-story farmhouse visible in the distance.

"Probably not, in fact, it's doubtful any of the Amish are involved, but you never know. Remember Corporal Fellows was a neighbor."

She tilted her head. "You're a neighbor too."

He nodded. "The difference is that you can trust me. I'm going back to post this afternoon to talk to Corporal Fellows's first sergeant. He worked in the same unit as your father. If you want to join me, I'd be happy to show you around Fort Rickman."

She hesitated for a moment and then nodded. "What time?"

Tyler glanced at his watch. "After lunch. Say one o'clock."

"I'll be ready."

Ty pulled his SUV to a stop in front of the large white home with the tall columns and yesteryear appeal. He stepped onto the driveway, rounded the car and climbed the porch. The front door opened before he had time to knock.

Carrie stood in the doorway, looking far too pretty in a flowing skirt and matching sweater. She had changed out of the rain-damp clothes she'd worn this morning. With a nod of greeting, she grabbed a jacket from the rack in the foyer and stepped onto the porch, closing the door behind her.

He reached for the coat and helped her slip it on. "The sun's out, but it's still chilly and damp."

"Thanks."

He pointed to the door. "It's locked, right?"

She nodded, then dug for keys in her purse. "But I'll engage the dead bolt." Flicking a worried glance at him, she added, "Just in case."

"That's right." Ty didn't want to belabor the point, but he was relieved that she understood the need for caution.

"Do you think Corporal Fellows's uniform may have made him a target?" she asked.

"You're concerned terrorism might have been involved?"

"Probably a long shot, but Senator Kingsley talks about some of the groups in the Middle East targeting young men and some women here in the States. Home-grown terrorism, lone wolf, whatever you want to call it, he believes we're going to see more acts of aggression and violence in the days to come."

Although Tyler hated to agree with the senator, he knew his assessment was right.

"I don't understand," Carrie continued, "how people can be brainwashed into thinking that killing has a greater good."

"They're looking for something to believe in, to give them an identity. A cause bigger than themselves. Without a good foundation of faith and morality, kids can confuse evil for good, especially when the message is coated with affirming rhetoric."

"Sounds as if you know what you're talking about."

He shrugged. "Our military is built on guys who want to do good and fight for a cause bigger than themselves. Thankfully they've found what all kids want—a stable foundation."

"Did you have that growing up?"

He laughed ruefully. "I had a strong-willed father who loved the Lord."

Tyler hadn't planned to talk about his childhood.

"I'm sure he's proud of you."

He hadn't expected her comment either. "Maybe he would have been, but he died when I was a kid."

"I'm sorry."

Opening the passenger door, he helped her into the seat. Before he slipped behind the wheel, he glanced at the nearby Amish farms and the expansive fields. His own life had been shattered years ago, which was probably why he had been drawn to the serenity of Amish Road. Just as had happened in his youth, death now threatened the peace and well-being of those who lived nearby.

No matter the reason for the crime, the murderer needed to be apprehended sooner rather than later. Otherwise the tranquil countryside would be torn apart, especially if the killer struck again.

FIVE

Fort Rickman, with its stately oaks and tall pine trees, wasn't what Carrie had expected. She had a preconceived notion of army posts filled with men in uniform marching across parade fields accompanied by flags and a band. Her false ideas had probably been the result of watching too many military movies as a kid that featured army heroes. Silly of her, but since she'd never known her father, she'd hoped the movies would help her understand the life he had lived.

Ty made a quick stop at CID headquarters and insisted she come into his office, which turned out to be a cubicle big enough for a desk and two chairs. He brought her coffee and asked for her to wait while he talked to one of the other agents about the case.

As she sipped the hot brew, she couldn't help noticing the lack of photos and other knickknacks on his desk. Everything was neat and tidy but unadorned with anything that smacked of family or gave her a clue about who Ty Zimmerman really was.

He returned and smiled. "Ready to go to your father's unit?"

She continued to be pleasantly surprised as they drove

across post. A stream meandered next to a walking trail that bordered a grassy knoll. The plentiful stands of trees and expansive green spaces reminded her of a national park. She'd been to Fort Meyer and Fort Belvoir in Virginia with the senator. Both posts were beautiful, but they weren't troop posts where soldiers trained for war. Somehow she hadn't expected anything as lush at Fort Rickman.

"It looks so peaceful," she said as they drove along a quiet two-lane road, overhung with a canopy of live oaks. "I expected dusty training areas with little or no vegetation."

He pointed left and then right. "The training areas stretch east and west on either side of the main post garrison. If you'd like, we could drive there."

She held up her hand. "That won't be necessary. I'm not even sure about stopping by my father's unit."

"I thought you wanted to know more about who he was and what was important to him."

"I do. It's just that…" She hesitated. "I don't know what to expect."

"Not to worry. From what I've heard, Sergeant Major Harris was well liked and well respected. I'm sure his men and colleagues will enjoy meeting you."

Tyler made a number of turns that eventually led to the engineer battalion. He pointed to a one-story brick building with a military flag hanging in front. To the side and rear were a number of three-story buildings.

"The taller structures are the barracks where the soldiers live. Battalion headquarters sits in the middle. That's where the commander works, along with his staff and the command sergeant major."

"Which was my father's position."

"That's correct. He was the ranking noncommissioned officer in the battalion."

All around them soldiers scurried from building to building. In the distance, she saw men standing in formation, and beside one of the barracks, military personnel were scrubbing trash cans. A soldier picked up a scrap of paper and tossed it in a nearby receptacle.

"Looks like everyone takes pride in maintaining the area."

"I'm sure your father stressed that to his men."

"They look so young."

"That's because they are, Carrie. Many of them are right out of high school."

"And going to war."

"If their unit is deployed."

Pulling to a stop, he again opened her door and then ushered her toward the headquarters.

Stepping inside, she was surprised when three soldiers, sitting at desks, all rose to greet her. She hadn't expected their manners or their welcoming smiles.

"Afternoon, ma'am," they said practically in unison. The tallest of the three men turned to Tyler. "How may I help you, sir?"

He showed his identification and gave his name and Carrie's. "I'd like to talk to Corporal Fellows's first sergeant."

"Yes, sir. That would be First Sergeant Baker. I'll call him and ask him to come to headquarters."

Tyler glanced at the office to the rear. The nameplate on the door read Command Sergeant Major Adams, evidently the man who had taken her father's position.

"Is the sergeant major in?" Tyler asked.

"Ah, no, sir. He's tied up at main post headquarters along with the commander."

"Ms. York is Sergeant Major Harris's daughter. I'm sure she'd appreciate seeing her father's former office, if you don't mind."

One of the other men came from around his desk. "Your dad was a fine man who did everything he could to help the troops. I'd be happy to show you around."

She followed the soldier into a corner office. A large desk sat in front of two windows. Three flags, including the American flag, stood nearby.

"Your father had the side wall filled with awards and commendations, ma'am. Close to thirty years on active duty. That's a career to be proud of, although I don't have to tell you."

She nodded, unable to think of anything to say that wouldn't expose her mixed emotions. "How did he treat the other men in the unit?" she asked, searching for something to say that wouldn't reveal her lack of knowledge of the military.

"He was by the book, if that's what you mean, ma'am, although the sergeant major liked to laugh. A deep bellowing sound that would fill a room. If you heard him laugh, you knew everything would be okay." Her guide suddenly looked embarrassed. "Forgive me, ma'am. I'm not telling you anything you didn't already know."

His statement took her aback. Confusion swept over her as it had too many times over the last twenty-some hours. If only she had heard her father's laughter.

Tears stung her eyes and a lump filled her throat. Not wanting the sergeant to realize her upset, she choked back her thanks and returned to the main area where Ty stood to the side talking to another man in uniform.

"I'll wait for you outside," she managed to say in passing as she hurried out the door and toward the car. Breathing in the fresh air, she stared at the pristine grounds that had been her father's life for close to thirty years. She knew so little about the military, and everything she thought she knew was proving to be wrong.

A breeze stirred the trees and made her hair swirl in front of her face. She pulled it behind her ears and wiped her hand across her cheeks. She needed to be strong, especially here, surrounded by men and women in uniform who sacrificed so much for the nation.

Carrie thought she had known who she was and where she'd come from. Since George Gates had called her, she had realized how her past had been clouded by her mother's lies. Regrettably the foundation upon which she'd built her life had been false.

Before arriving at Tyler's car, someone shouted her name. She turned, seeing a soldier, late thirties, blond hair visible under his beret. He ran toward her.

"Ma'am, one of the men said you were Sergeant Major Harris's daughter."

"That's correct."

He held out his hand. "Sergeant Oliver, ma'am. Pleased to meet you."

She returned the handshake.

"I was with your father in the Middle East and served with him here at Fort Rickman. His death was hard on all of us who knew him. If there's anything I can do, don't hesitate to ask."

"Thank you, Sergeant."

"You've heard about the ceremony at the end of the month for Freemont veterans?"

"My father's lawyer mentioned that a plaque would be unveiled honoring my father."

"Yes, ma'am. The unit's putting together a slide slow that will be played during the ceremony. The photos highlight the work our soldiers do within the civilian community. I want to add a portion about your father since he's being honored."

"That's very thoughtful."

"It's the least I can do to recognize his contribution. He did a lot of good for a lot of people, but then I don't have to tell you. Although I've got a number of pictures that the Public Affairs Office has taken, I'd like to include a few more. Any chance I could borrow some of the snapshots he had at home?"

"He has an office in the rear of the house. I could search through his papers."

The sergeant handed her his business card. "Call me if you find some that might work. I can pick them up anytime."

"Give me a day or two, Sergeant."

"That's fine, ma'am, and I don't want to pressure you."

"You're not, it's just that I've got a lot to take in when it comes to my father. Being on post today seems to be affecting me emotionally."

"Grief is hard, ma'am."

She appreciated the sergeant's understanding. Turning to regain her composure, Carrie gazed at the various military structures, surprised to see a wooden building with a steeple and cross on the next block. "Is that a church?"

Oliver nodded. "Yes, ma'am. It's Soldiers Chapel. The sergeant major's funeral was held there."

"Not in Freemont?"

"He worshipped on-post, ma'am, and as I understand it, he requested to have his service at the chapel."

When Carrie had met with George Gates this morning, she had expressed her desire to see her father's grave, although she hadn't thought to ask about the funeral and where it had taken place. The realization hung heavy on her shoulders. That should have been one of her first questions. "Do you know where he was buried?"

"Freemont Cemetery. It's on Freemont Road, which connects the post to town. You probably passed it on your way to Fort Rickman."

"I'm sure we did." But her mind had been on other things rather than burying the dead.

"I wasn't able to attend the graveside service," Oliver admitted. "The men said the chaplain did a good job."

Oliver glanced back at the headquarters. "I won't take any more of your time, and I'd better get back to work."

"Thank you, Sergeant. If you see Special Agent Zimmerman inside, would you mind telling him I plan to visit the chapel?"

"Will do, ma'am."

The sun peered through the clouds and warmed Carrie's back as she hurried toward the chapel. A group of soldiers doubled-timed along the nearby road, the rhythmic cadence of their Jody calls sounding in the quiet afternoon. Under other circumstances, she would have smiled at the lighthearted jingle about military life that set the pace as the soldiers ran in formation, but at this moment and after everything that had happened, the slap of their boots on the pavement reminded her of the long line of men and women who had gone to war.

Today their sacrifice seemed especially hard to bear. While she had been getting her degree and living the good life, so many had shipped off to the Middle East. Some hadn't returned home. Others had been maimed, wounded or psychologically or emotionally scarred.

Greater love hath no man...

The words from scripture played through her mind in time with the passing unit.

Arriving at the chapel, she climbed the steps, pulled open the glass door and stepped into the small narthex. Religious magazines and pamphlets hung on racks to the left. A door on the right led to an office. Seeing no one inside, she continued on into the sacristy, where she was welcomed by reflected sunlight that angled through the stained glass windows.

The scent of candle wax hung heavy in the air. She inhaled deeply and recalled the few times in her youth that she'd attended Sunday services. A relationship with the Lord hadn't been one of her mother's priorities. Regrettably Carrie had followed in her mother's less-than-faithful footsteps.

She slipped into a pew midway down the aisle and closed her eyes. Pictures flashed through her mind of the bigger-than-life hero she had envisioned in her youth. That make-believe dad had been repeatedly berated by her mother who had little to say that was positive about the military. Landing a job with the senator had further eroded any idealized concept that remained of her father.

Opening her eyes, she gazed at the cross hanging on the wall behind the altar, knowing she had hardened her heart not only to her parents, but also to the Lord.

Instead of embracing Christ's message of love and forgiveness, she had turned her focus inward, to her own self-serving needs. Just like many of the people with whom she worked with in Washington, the emphasis was on their own lives and not the true well-being of the nation.

Could she have been so wrong?

A door opened. She turned to see two men in uniform enter the chapel. The older of the two—a man in his forties—nodded before stepping inside the office. The younger man, early twenties, followed.

Feeling suddenly ill at ease, she left the pew and headed for the door, which opened again. Ty entered the chapel, his gaze filled with question as if he wondered why she was seeking solace in this place of worship.

Glancing into the office, he raised his hand in greeting. "Afternoon, Chaplain."

The older man met him in the narthex. The two shook hands. "Good to see you, Tyler. I have a feeling your visit involves Corporal Fellows. Terrible shame. We've lost too many soldiers in the Middle East. Tragic some succumb to violence in our own country."

"Yes, sir." Tyler introduced Carrie to the chaplain.

She accepted his handshake. "Nice to meet you, sir. I'm Carolyn York. I believe you officiated at my father's funeral. Sergeant Major Harris."

The chaplain's square face softened. "Less than two weeks ago. My sympathies. Your father was a good man with a strong faith. Knowing him was an honor."

She tried to smile, but the twisted feelings of inadequacy tangled around her heart. "I didn't know my father, and only learned of his death a few days ago. I'm trying to piece together a picture of who he was."

The chaplain nodded as if he understood. "Be assured that he loved the Lord."

"Which seems strange for a man of war."

"A man of peace," the chaplain corrected. "The military protects and defends against forces of evil that threaten our way of life. Our soldiers provide a deterrent against aggression. God would not have us stand idly by when evil looms so close and threatens those who cannot protect themselves."

"I never thought of it that way."

The chaplain turned to the younger man and introduced his assistant, Jason Jones. "Can you find one of the programs from Sergeant Major Harris's funeral for Ms. York?"

"Yes, sir." The soldier rummaged in a file cabinet and then handed her a folded program. A cross with lilies adorned the front.

She turned it over and stared at the photo of the man in uniform pictured on the back cover, the father she had never known.

"Thank you for your kind words, Chaplain. I'd like to visit his grave site at some point."

"Of course." He turned to Tyler, who had remained silent. "You know the Freemont Cemetery. It's not far from post if you go out the main gate."

Tyler nodded. "On the left off Freemont Road."

"That's correct. Enter the cemetery and make a right at the dead end. The grave sits on a small knoll around the first bend. You'll see the newly covered grave about twenty feet from the road on your right. The sergeant major had chosen the grave site just a few days prior to his death."

"Was there some urgency in selecting a burial spot?" Carrie asked. "My father wasn't that old. Had he been ill?"

"He told me that he thought about selling his property and moving to Florida, but reconsidered. Evidently his ancestors had settled around here in the 1800s. Once he made the decision to stay in Freemont, he made arrangements for his burial, although I don't think he realized how timely his decision would be."

"Did he ever talk about other family members?" she asked.

"He mentioned a daughter he had never seen." The chaplain's gaze was filled with compassion. "I presume that's you, Carrie. But he had no other family."

"Thank you, Chaplain." She nodded to the soldier who had found the funeral program before she turned to Tyler. "If we have time, I'd like to stop at the cemetery."

"Of course." He shook hands with the chaplain. "Good seeing you, sir."

Stepping outside, she glanced at the building where her father had worked. A soldier, yet a man of God and a man of peace, which went counter to what she had believed about him for the past few years. Pulling her coat around her neck, she and Tyler hurried back to the car. He opened the door, and she slipped into the passenger seat, still struggling with both confusion and grief. She had come to Fort Rickman hoping to get answers as to who her father was, but what she had learned only bewildered her more. A good man, a role model to his soldiers, a man who loved the Lord?

He'd chosen his grave site just days prior to his death and had been killed in a fall nearly two weeks before another soldier from his unit was tragically and heinously murdered on her father's property. Surely the two deaths had to be intertwined. But how?

Tyler sensed Carrie's tension as they left Fort Rickman and headed north along Freemont Road. She'd been hit with a lot of information about her father, all good, but probably hard to sort through, as well.

"I'm glad you met the chaplain, Carrie. He's a good man. Seems he thought highly of your father."

"Thank you for taking me to post. I…I don't think I could have found his unit on my own."

"The cemetery isn't far, but I know you're probably worn out. Do you want to stop now or would you rather return another day?"

"Now, if you have time."

"It's not a problem."

"What did you find out from the first sergeant?" she asked.

"Only that Corporal Fellows did his job, although he kept to himself. The first sergeant will talk to the guys in his platoon and see if anyone knows anything about his private life."

"Did the rental situation concern you?"

"Only if your father was Fellows's boss. The CID learned Fellows hadn't been here long and arrived well after your father's time on active duty ended."

"I wonder if they were friends or ever did things together. I keep thinking it's more than a coincidence that they both died in the same area so closely together."

Tyler had to agree, but he knew investigations could change direction in the blink of an eye when the right piece of information was revealed. The CID was looking into Fellows's past. The Freemont police were investigating the murder from the civilian angle, and Tyler was keeping tabs on the newly found daughter whose arrival in Freemont corresponded with Fellows's death.

A coincidence?
Maybe yes.
Or maybe no.

SIX

Tyler turned into the cemetery and followed the chaplain's directions. Seeing the newly covered grave, he pulled to the side of the road. Carrie opened the passenger door and sighed as she stepped from the car.

Together, they walked to where dried flower arrangements still covered a mound of soil. A small stone indicated the number of the grave but not the name of the deceased buried there.

She stared at the ground for a long moment, her voice a whisper when she finally spoke. "I need to ask George Gates about a monument."

"The military will provide a marker. We can contact the funeral home and inquire about what's been arranged."

"If a marker hasn't been ordered, it's something I could do." She glanced at Tyler. "Something to show deference to my father."

"That would be very appropriate, Carrie, and would honor his memory."

"A memory I don't have." She clasped her hands. "I don't even know how to pray for him."

Tyler lowered his eyes, sensing Carrie's anguish and

wishing he could comfort her. From deep inside, words sprang. "God bless Carrie's father. Draw him close to You in the everlasting life where You dwell, O Lord. Amen."

"Thank you, Tyler." She offered a weak smile. "Your words were far more meaningful than anything I could manage. Ever since Gates called and told me about my father, I've felt empty and unable to pray. Not that prayer was part of my life before, but the void has gotten bigger these last few days."

"God knows how you feel, Carrie."

"Does He?" She shook her head. "I don't think He's happy with the type of person I've become. I'm sure my father would wonder about my faith and lack of trust in the Lord. I never thought finding information about the man I wanted to know my whole life would make me so conflicted."

The low whine of a car engine turned Tyler's attention to the crest of the hill where a dark sedan pulled to a stop. The driver of the car extended something through his open window and raised it to his eyes.

Tyler's heart stopped as realization hit like a two-by-four. He grabbed Carrie's shoulders and threw her to the ground behind the mound of turned earth and dried flower arrangements. She gasped. In less than a heartbeat, the bullet whizzed past them.

"Stay down," Tyler warned.

Tires squealed in the distance.

Raising his head, he searched the hill, then flicked his gaze around the surrounding area, looking for any sign of the shooter. "The car's gone."

"Who was it?" Carrie moaned as she worked to free herself from under Tyler's hold.

"Sorry." He scooted aside, all the while keeping his eyes on the hillside.

Satisfied the shooter and car had both left the area, Tyler stood and helped Carrie to her feet. "Let's get back to my vehicle. Hurry."

Keeping his hand on the small of her back, he ushered her forward. Once they both were in the car, he headed out of the cemetery and onto Freemont Road, where he reached for his cell and called Officer Inman.

"I'm driving Carrie back to her father's house," Tyler quickly told the law enforcement officer. "The shot came from a dark sedan parked on the crest of the hill. See if one of your men can find tire prints or anything the shooter might have left behind. You know how to contact me. My cell's on."

Disconnecting, he glanced at Carrie. Tears filled her eyes, and although her shoulders were braced against the seat, her hands trembled and her sweet face was pulled tight with fear.

"You're okay. The person fled." Tyler rubbed his hand over hers, hoping to offer reassurance.

She dabbed at her eyes. "Did…did you see the shooter's face?"

"Negative. Just the car and rifle."

"Who knew I was at the cemetery?"

"It could have been anyone, Carrie."

"What about the chaplain?" she asked.

"I don't think Chaplain Simmons is involved, but questioning his assistant might be prudent."

Tyler called Everett at CID headquarters and filled him in on what had happened. "Send someone to Soldiers Chapel ASAP. Chaplain Simmons doesn't worry me, but he can provide information about his assistant.

See if Jason Jones remained at the chapel. If not, he could have followed us to the cemetery."

"I'm on it," Everett said before he disconnected.

"I mentioned wanting to see my father's grave to George Gates," Carrie admitted, once Tyler placed his phone on the console.

"Did you tell him you planned to stop by the cemetery today?"

She shook her head. "I merely said that I wanted to at some point before returning to DC."

But that might have been enough. The tire could have been tampered with when Carrie was visiting the lawyer. Easy enough for Gates to have an accomplice who handled the dirty work. Tyler needed to know more about the lawyer and how involved he was in the sergeant major's business.

Carrie felt as if she were having a bad dream that kept getting darker and darker. She wanted to pinch herself and wake up back in time, before George Gates's call, before she knew about her real father, before she had driven to Freemont and gotten involved with a murder investigation.

Thinking of all that had happened, she shivered.

"Cold?" Tyler reached for the heater control on the dashboard.

"Not physically, but I feel cold inside and empty, as I mentioned at the cemetery before someone tried to kill me. If not the chaplain's assistant, then who fired the shot?"

"The same person who took the lug nuts from your tire. He wants to scare you."

"He succeeded." She laughed ruefully. "But I'm grateful he isn't a better shot."

"He only fired once, Carrie, which means he probably had no intention of injuring you."

"That's doesn't reassure me. Besides, how can you be certain that he wasn't aiming at you?"

Tyler almost smiled. "All of us in law enforcement have plenty of people who would like to do us harm, but the lug nuts weren't taken from my car. You're the target."

"Which doesn't bode well for my staying in Freemont."

"Could anyone from DC have followed you here? Is the senator working on a new bill or resolution that has a lot of opposition? An angry constituent might turn his ire against you, especially if he had trouble accessing the senator."

"Doesn't it seem more than a stretch to have something the senator does in Washington impact me here in Georgia?"

"Yet it's worth considering. Have you had problems in DC?"

"A few prank phone calls. Some tweets and Facebook comments that are hateful, but nothing like this. Nothing that ended in violence."

"Do you remember the names of the people on social media?"

"It was months ago, Tyler. I really don't think they have any bearing on what's been happening here. Free speech, remember? Folks can say anything they want. This is different."

Different and deadly, she wanted to add.

Tyler lowered his speed as they neared the Freemont city limits.

"Let's stop by the lawyer's office and tell George Gates about the missing lug nuts," Tyler suggested. "He'll deny knowledge, even if he was involved, but I'd like to see his reaction when you tell him."

Approaching the center of town, Tyler turned onto the side road and pulled into the parking lot behind the law office. They entered the building through the rear door. A woman sat at a desk in the outer office that had been vacant earlier today.

She looked up as they approached. The nameplate on her desk read Flo Beacon.

Carrie introduced herself. "I was here earlier today and need to talk to George Gates again. Is he in his office?"

Flo was middle-aged with overly made-up eyes and a heavy smear of blush that darkened her full cheeks. "You're Jeffrey Harris's daughter?"

Carrie nodded. "That's right. Did you know my father?"

"Of course. He stopped by the office a number of times, especially a few weeks before his death." Her eyes widened. "I'm sorry about your dad. My condolences."

"Thank you."

"George left the office a short while ago, Ms. York. Can you come back in the morning?"

"Probably not. I wanted to find out if anyone strange had been hanging around the office earlier today. My tires were tampered with when my car was parked in the lot out back."

"Oh my." Flo patted her chest. "I'm so sorry. We've never had any problem before. I'll let George know. Did you contact the police?"

"They know about the situation." Tyler stepped closer to the desk. "You said Sergeant Major Harris visited the law office frequently leading up to his death. Was he working on his will or estate planning?"

Flo batted her eyes. "I'm not sure, nor am I at liberty to discuss his legal dealings."

"We wouldn't want you to divulge anything you shouldn't," Carried reassured the receptionist.

"And I wouldn't," Flo said with a smile. "But it is fortunate for you that your father didn't sell the property a few weeks ago when a buyer came forward."

"For the entire property or just the house?" Carrie asked.

Flo shrugged. "I thought the entire estate was for sale."

"Do you know who made the offer?" Tyler asked.

"There were whispers around town of an outside development corporation that was interested in the land. You might want to talk to Nelson Quinn. He's a local real estate agent. Seems I heard he was involved in the offer."

Carrie glanced at Tyler, then back at Flo. "What time do you expect Mr. Gates tomorrow?"

"He's usually at his desk by nine in the morning. I'll tell him you stopped by."

Before they left through the rear door, Flo called out to them. "In case you're interested in local history, the Freemont Museum is open this afternoon. If you haven't been there yet, you might enjoy learning a bit more about our local area."

Tyler glanced back at her. "I didn't know there was a museum."

"It's newly opened. The Historical Society has been gathering objects for display. A lady named Yvonne runs the place. The sergeant major donated a few things from the Harris home."

"It's close by?" Carrie asked.

"Across the street in the old train station." Flo glanced

at her watch. "It's open from two until five each afternoon. You've got about an hour until it closes for the day."

"Let's pay the museum a visit," Carrie said when they stepped outside.

Tyler's phone rang. He glanced at the screen. "It's Everett."

Lifting the cell to his ear, he said, "Did you talk to the men?" He nodded. "Right."

Carrie waited, eager to hear what the other CID agent had learned.

When Tyler disconnected, he turned to her. "The chaplain vouched for his assistant. The men had been working on a new program for married military families, along with two of the sergeants from the engineer battalion. No one had left the office since we were there last. Everett's running background checks, but he's confident they couldn't have driven to the cemetery and fired the shot."

Carrie sighed. "Which takes us back to square one."

Tyler pointed down the street. "Let's wait to tour the museum. There's a real estate office on the next block. I'd like to see if Nelson Quinn works there and find out what he knows about the development corporation."

A receptionist welcomed them to Freemont Real Estate and quickly explained that Mr. Quinn was out of town and not expected back for the next five to seven days.

Carrie couldn't help feeling frustrated at another delay. If they continued to find doors closed, the investigation would take forever.

"Do you know anything about an out-of-town corporation that was interested in buying the old antebellum home on Amish Road?" Tyler asked the receptionist.

"A beautiful house," she noted. "I'm not aware of any offer on the home, but I'll tell Mr. Quinn to call you when he returns to work."

Tyler provided his contact information before he and Carrie walked outside.

"I'm beginning to think we'll never learn who's responsible for the attacks."

"Police investigations take time, Carrie. The local cops and the CID are working on the case. Something will break."

She didn't share his enthusiasm, but she tried to appear encouraged as they crossed the street to the small depot that had been turned into a visitors center.

A sign pointed them to the Historic Freemont Museum in the rear where a number of freestanding glass cases displayed an assortment of artifacts and historic memorabilia. Yvonne, the visitors center greeter, who doubled as the museum's docent, welcomed them. When Carrie mentioned her father's donation, the woman directed them to a glass showcase near one of the side windows.

A number of antique farm implements and a few kitchen items were tagged as having been gifts from Jeffrey Harris, along with two sheets of stationery, yellowed with age. The swirled handwriting on the heavy paper was beautifully scripted but hard to read. Carrie leaned over the display case to get a clearer view.

Tyler glanced over her shoulder. His nearness stirred a sensation deep within her that Carrie couldn't explain. Not anxiety or fear but unsettling just the same. She scooted sideways to give herself space as she studied the fluid script.

"My Dearest Son," the missive began. The letter recounted local farm activities as well as the health and well-being of family members.

"Word has come to us about the Northern forces' advancement," the writer of the letter continued. "We will stand firm and be vigilant, yet all the while taking precautions and preparing lest they come this far south. As we discussed before you left, dear son, your mother and I have secured our family treasures from enemy hands and have placed them where they cannot be pillaged or found. I have left a map to the whereabouts of our precious items and worldly wealth in my desk, which I pray to God you will find and not the Northerners. Even should they surround the house and take me captive, you have my solemn word, my dear son, that I will fight to the death to protect our land and our treasure.

"Your affectionate father,

"Jefferson Harris."

"Jefferson must be a distant relative." She glanced at Tyler. "Interesting that he mentions treasure and wealth."

"Which could be anything of worth to a family in those days. Actually your father's gift of the letter and farm and kitchen implements to the museum was very generous."

Tyler's comment gave her pause. She glanced at the number of objects in the Harris collection. "You're right. My father's gift was generous."

Together she and Tyler viewed the other items on display that chronicled the change in the area from a land of cotton fields to small farms that now dotted the countryside. Old photos showed Fort Rickman's beginning days as a training camp for soldiers heading to Europe in the 1940s. A series of photos and graphs chronicled the recent growth to the area owing to the fort's expansion, along with short write-ups about the friendly partnership between the military and civilian communities. A newer section of the small but informative museum mentioned the arrival of the Amish families and the positive role they played in the development of the outlying areas.

When Yvonne politely reminded them that the museum would soon close for the night, Carrie and Tyler said their farewells and hurried outside. Eyeing the end-of-the-day traffic flow, Carrie saw something that made her heart lurch. A military guy in uniform pulled out of the law firm parking lot just as she and Tyler were ready to cross the street.

She tapped Tyler's arms. "Isn't that the chaplain's assistant?"

Tyler followed her gaze and nodded. "You're right. I wonder what Jason Jones is doing in town."

"Making an appointment with George Gates?"

"Maybe, but why would a soldier need a civilian lawyer when the military provides JAG services on post? The timing has me concerned. He must have left Soldiers Chapel soon after Everett's visit."

They crossed the street, and Tyler pointed to the law office. "Let's pay Flo Beacon another visit and see what she can tell us about Jason."

Carrie reached for the door and found it locked. The hours of operations on the wall read Mon–Fri, 9 AM–5 PM.

"We're not making progress," she said with a sigh.

"Not yet, but something will break soon. I'm sure of it."

Once they settled into his car, Tyler called post. Everett's phone went to voice mail, and Tyler left a message about seeing the chaplain's assistant.

"Jason Jones needs more scrutiny," Tyler warned. "Let me know if anything surfaces from your background checks."

Disconnecting, he glanced at Carrie. "If the soldier is involved, Everett should be able to pick up the trail."

"At least we know he didn't fire the shot at the cemetery."

Tyler nodded. "But I'm still concerned about his connection with George Gates."

Carrie was concerned, as well. What was happening in Freemont, and why did it involve her?

Traffic was heavy as Tyler drove through Freemont, but it eased once they turned onto the country road that led to the Amish community. As they passed the spot of Carrie's accident, she turned to stare at the ditch.

"Have you heard from the mechanic?" Tyler asked.

"Not yet. Maybe he's having trouble finding a tire that matches the other three."

"You might want to call him."

"I'll do that in the morning."

The rolling hills and fertile fields were such a stark contrast from the hustle and bustle of small-town Freemont they had just left. Transferring back to the States after three years overseas, Tyler had yearned for the peace and calm he had grown to enjoy in rural Germany. He'd been drawn to the Amish community when he learned of a house for rent. Now the serenity of the area had been disrupted with the murder. Maybe he had picked the wrong location.

Turning onto Amish Road, he studied the farmhouses that dotted the area. Wash hung on clotheslines and blew in the breeze. A buggy passed them on the opposite side of the road. The *clip-clop* of the horse's hooves on the pavement served as a not-so-subtle reminder of the differences between the *plain* and *English* ways of life. The bearded man holding the reins raised his hand in greeting as the buggy passed.

Had Carrie's father found respite in the Amish community with the rolling hills and bucolic farms? Or had he taken up residence in the old homestead for another reason?

Approaching the Harris home, Tyler turned into the driveway and pulled the car to a stop at the side of the house. A man appeared, seemingly from thin air. He was tall with broad shoulders, a thick beard and a black hat.

Alarmed by his presence and worried about Carrie's safety, Tyler hopped from the car. "May I help you?"

"I am Simon Plank. My son said you questioned his care of the chickens."

Instantly relieved, Tyler stretched out his hand. "You're Eli's father?"

"Yah." The man accepted the handshake.

Carrie stepped out of the car and moved closer. "I am grateful for your son's help, Mr. Plank. Special Agent Zimmerman was concerned about finding a stranger on the property this morning. You've probably heard about the soldier who died here last night."

Simon nodded. "I learned of this today. My son had nothing to do with the dead soldier or any of them."

"By any of them, do you mean soldiers from Fort Rickman?" Tyler asked.

"Not from the fort, but from someplace nearby. They try to talk our young boys into doing things that God forbids."

Tyler looked at Carrie. "What type of things, sir?"

"Playing cards and movies that are not suitable for anyone to watch, especially for the young."

"Sir, can you give me the names of the people who have approached the boys?"

"I do not have names. I have only heard about what has happened. I do not want this to happen to my boy."

"I'm in complete agreement. If Eli hears of anyone upsetting the youth in this community, please tell me. I'll personally find the soldiers involved and talk to them and have their superiors counsel them, if necessary."

"What about the care of the chickens?" Simon asked. "Eli helped Isaac Lapp as a favor while they were gone."

Glancing at Carrie, he added, "My son said you wanted to pay him to do the job."

"That's right. As you probably know, my father died a little less than two weeks ago. I could use Eli's help, and I will pay him for his work."

"The job is still available?"

"Yes, I'd enjoy having his help," Carrie said.

"*Gut*. Eli will save the money. He is young and dreams with his eyes open."

Tyler smiled. "Most kids do, but I don't think you have to worry about Eli."

"A father always wants his child to follow God's way. That is my desire." He nodded to Carrie. "I will tell him he can accept the job."

After a nod of farewell, the Amish farmer crossed the road and walked toward his house. Simon's words played through Tyler's mind. *"A father wants his son to follow God's way."*

Tyler's own father would have said the same thing. He had been strict, almost to an extreme, but also committed to the Lord. His dad had expected Tyler to embrace the beliefs he held dear, yet his tragic death had sent Tyler's world into chaos. How could a boy continue to believe in a God Who had allowed such darkness into his young life? To Tyler's way of thinking, God had abandoned him when his father died.

Or had Tyler been the one to close his heart to the Lord?

"Are the Amish naive about their faith, or do they have it right?" Tyler stared into the distance and watched as Simon entered his farmhouse.

Carrie sighed. "I'm not sure."

Hearing the fatigue in her voice, he touched her arms. "I know you're tired. Go inside. Lock the doors and windows. I'll stay outside and keep watch for a while."

She shook her head. "I appreciate your thoughtfulness, but that's not necessary. As you mentioned at the cemetery, the shooter tried to scare me instead of doing me harm. Go home, Tyler. Get some rest. I'll call you if I hear anything or become fearful."

"I can drive you to the garage tomorrow if your car is ready. Or if you want to talk to Gates."

"Aren't you going to post?"

"At some point, but I can also work from home." He didn't mention that he'd been tasked to ensure her safety and to find out if she had additional information about the case.

When she unlocked the door, Bailey bounded outside and barked with enthusiasm.

"You've been cooped up for too long," Carrie laughed. "Sorry, boy."

His tail wagged as he paused for her to rub his neck, then scurried to greet Tyler.

"Hey there, Bailey. What have you been up to?"

The dog barked playfully. He scampered around the yard before bounding across the road.

Carrie called to him, but Bailey ignored her. Instead he raced to where Eli walked along the road, coming back to the Harris home.

"Looks like your new hired hand is ready to get started on his job," Tyler said with a smile.

"With Bailey's help."

The dog and teenager crossed the road and approached where Tyler and Carrie stood. Eli nodded in greeting. "My *Datt* said you still want me to care for the chickens."

"Yes, thank you, Eli. If Bailey gets underfoot I can call him inside."

The boy scratched Bailey's ears. "He likes to help, and the chickens do not worry about him when he is outside the fence."

The boy and dog walked toward the barn to get the feed. Carrie turned as if ready to go inside.

Much as Tyler didn't want to leave her, he said good-bye and climbed into his SUV for the short drive home. He pulled into the driveway of his house and killed the engine. As he exited the car, he glanced at Eli and Bailey sauntering toward the chicken coop, relieved the day would end better than it had begun.

Once at his door, Tyler wiped his feet on the mat. Before he turned the key, he heard Eli running back to the Harris house.

Even at this distance, Tyler could tell something was wrong. Bailey followed close behind the boy with his head down and tail between his legs.

Tyler ran across the green space between the two

homes. Carrie stepped onto the porch, her face drawn as she watched the boy run toward her.

"Chickens," Eli called. "Ten of them. Blood. Feathers. Their necks have been broken. They are dead."

SEVEN

Tyler and Officer Inman inspected the chicken coop while Eli sat on the front porch with Bailey. Carrie fixed the teenager a glass of lemonade and brought cookies for him to eat, insisting that he stay close until Tyler and the police officer finished checking the damage.

Glancing at the police car in her driveway, she was glad Inman hadn't sounded his siren or flashed his lights. She didn't want the memory of last night to return. Had it only been twenty-four hours since she arrived in Freemont?

So much had happened and none of it good.

"Have another cookie," she encouraged Eli.

"I dropped the feed bucket. It spilled. I should not be so wasteful."

"That's not a concern, Eli. I can get more feed. I'm more worried about you. I know seeing the chickens upset you."

"Why would someone do that to innocent animals?"

"I don't know," she answered truthfully.

"My *Datt* said someone was killed here last night."

She nodded. "A soldier who lived in a trailer in the woods. Did you know him?"

Eli's eyes widened. "A friend of mine saw two soldiers

arguing on the hill. He stayed back so they would not see him. He said the soldiers were angry, and he feared for his own safety."

"When was that?"

The boy shrugged. "Maybe two weeks ago."

"Who's your friend?" she pressed.

"I should not say things that he told me."

"The police need to know. The arguing soldiers could have been involved with the soldier's death last night. You wouldn't be wrong to share your friend's name."

The boy thought for a long moment, then shook his head again. "I cannot."

"Does your friend live near here?"

"Not far."

"Had he seen the soldiers before?"

"Not my friend, but I have heard other boys talk about the soldiers."

Tyler and Officer Inman approached the porch.

Carrie stood. "Did you find anything that might point to who did it?"

"I'm afraid not," Inman said with a discouraged shake of his head. "The wire on the side of the coop was cut. More than likely, the person knew you weren't home since he acted in daylight."

The officer glanced at the neighbor's house. "They must have known the Lapps were gone too."

Carrie shared what Eli had told her.

Tyler glanced down at the teenager. "If you won't tell us your friend's name, Eli, then encourage him to come forward. The information could help us find some bad people who have hurt others. Do you understand?"

The boy bit his lip and nodded.

"Go home, Eli, before your father gets worried about

you," Officer Inman said. "But if you think of anything else, tell Ms. York or Special Agent Zimmerman. They'll pass the information on to me."

Eli downed the lemonade and looked at the plate of cookies.

"I'll get a plastic bag, and you can take the rest of the cookies home," Carrie suggested.

"That is too much. May I have one more?"

"Of course. And come back anytime, Eli."

"I will clean the coop before I go."

Tyler held up his hand to stop the boy. "I'll take care of the cleanup. You can come back tomorrow and feed and water the chickens that weren't hurt."

"I will." He took a cookie.

"Take another one," Carrie encouraged.

He nodded his thanks, took the second cookie and hurried home.

Tyler turned to the police officer. "We need to find this guy."

"He seems to be everywhere."

"As if he knows my schedule." Carrie shivered and wrapped her arms around her waist. "Could my phone be telling him where to find me?"

"Might be smart to turn off your cell when you're not using it," Inman suggested. "You can't be sure about this person…" He hesitated. "Or persons. They could be making good guesses. You said the soldier in the chaplain's office heard that you planned to stop at the cemetery. Then you saw him at George Gate's office?"

"After we visited the museum. The lawyer's receptionist mentioned that my father had donated items I wanted to see."

"Hate to tell you, but I haven't had a chance to stop

by the museum. It's only been open a short time. One of the ladies in town did most of the work on getting the project off the ground. What did you find?"

"Some old farm and kitchen tools and a letter that talked about family treasure."

Inman nodded knowingly. "Folks have been spreading rumors about treasure since I was a kid. A Southerner's worst nightmare was having the Union soldiers pillage his farm and home. Hiding valuables was universally done south of the Mason-Dixon Line." He scratched his chin. "Thing is, we don't know what was hidden. Everyone dreams big. Talk is there were gold coins, but that's probably not the case."

"Have you uncovered anything new on Corporal Fellows's death?" Tyler stated the question everyone wanted answered.

Inman sighed. "I'm afraid not. His trailer was clean. The only thing we found were some shrubs that needed to be planted around his trailer."

Carrie gazed at the farmland that paralleled the road and stretched all around her father's property. Her property. She failed to think of it as such.

"I'm heading back to headquarters," Officer Inman said. "Keep your eyes open. No telling what this guy or group of men might try next, so be cautious." He pointed to Tyler. "You've got this guy next door. Don't hesitate to call him."

Once the officer had left, Tyler touched her arm. "I'll hang around outside for a while."

"I was thinking about fixing something for dinner. Maybe burgers and a salad. I've got more than enough for you to join me, if you don't already have plans."

He smiled. "Burgers sound great. I saw a grill behind the house, if you want some help."

"Perfect. Thanks." She opened the door and motioned him to follow her inside. Opening her purse, she drew out her phone and placed it on the counter.

"Is your GPS turned off?" Tyler asked.

"I can't remember if I ever turned it on."

Tyler stepped closer. He picked up the cell and handed it back to her. "The GPS would pinpoint your location whenever you post on social media. Check your settings. You should be able to find it."

She sifted through a number of screens. "Here it is. No, it's off."

"That's good. You might want to turn the cell off when you're not using it, as Officer Inman mentioned, just as another precaution."

"I'll do that after dinner. I'm waiting for a phone call from my office."

"Have you had any time to work on the senator's speech?" he asked, following her into the kitchen.

"Not yet. I'd hoped to get some guidance from him first."

"Who's he speaking to?"

"A veteran's group."

"Then he probably wants his antimilitary rhetoric toned down a bit."

"He's not antimilitary, Tyler. It's more about spending and the defense budget."

"You can't have a well-trained military without supplies and technology and battle-fighting capabilities, Carrie. The senator likes to pretend he stands with the military, when he undermines them by cutting their funding."

"The budget has grown far too large."

"I agree, but look at social spending within the US. The national defense budget pales in comparison."

"Maybe we should change the subject," she finally said, pulling a package of ground chuck from the refrigerator. "Or agree to disagree."

"Stay away from politics and religion, right?"

"That might be wise."

"While you make the burgers, I'll bring the grill around to the kitchen door."

Tyler stepped outside and then glanced back to her. "First, I'd better bury the chickens and get the coop cleaned out."

"I feel indebted."

"Don't. One of the foster homes I lived in was in the country. I know my way around a barnyard."

"Thank you, Tyler." She watched him walk away, heading for the chicken coop and a job she didn't know if she could have handled. Tyler helped her in so many ways, but then, she was an assignment to him. He needed to stay close and ensure that she didn't get hurt. At least, that was what he had probably been told. For a moment, she wished their relationship could be something more.

Grabbing another hunk of ground beef, she forced herself to think of other things rather than the handsome special agent who was off-limits. Too soon, she'd be driving back to DC and her job. She didn't have time to get involved with someone in Georgia, especially a special agent who was all business. Bottom line, she needed to be strong and keep up her guard, especially when Tyler was around.

Tyler walked away from Carrie before he could say something that he'd later regret, something about how she looked at home in the kitchen and how having dinner with her this evening sounded special.

Carrie was a city girl. She had undoubtedly worked hard to land the position with Senator Kingsley, even if Tyler didn't espouse the politician's beliefs. Once she decided what to do with her father's estate, she'd head back to the hustle and bustle of Washington and leave her antebellum roots behind.

Finding a shovel in the barn and a small cardboard box, he placed the remains in the box and buried it in the wooded area. He fed the remaining chickens, ran fresh water into their trough and repaired the fence to keep them safe from animal predators. If only he could keep Carrie safe from the two-legged kind who kept attacking her.

Once finished, he tapped on her kitchen door. His chest hitched when she peered outside, looking flushed.

"I'll shower and return shortly," he said, taking a step back to distance himself from her alluring charm. "Is there anything you still need?"

"Just some charcoal, if you have extra."

"I've got a full bag from the last time I stopped in the commissary."

After a quick shower, Tyler returned wearing khaki trousers and a button-down-collar shirt and a pullover fleece. He carried a ten-pound bag of Match Light charcoal and arranged the charcoal in the grill. As the fire caught, he knocked on her door.

"Thanks again for the invitation," he said when she invited him inside. She'd done something to her hair that made it curl over her shoulders and had slipped into slacks and a colorful long-sleeve blouse.

"The burgers are ready for the grill whenever the fire's hot."

He laughed when he saw the plate piled high. "Looks like enough to feed an army."

She smiled. "Did I overdo?"

"I'll eat two."

"We'll have leftovers."

Was that another invitation?

Once the charcoal was hot, Tyler grabbed the plate and headed out the door. Bailey followed on his heels but quickly bounded toward the Amish house next door.

Eight-year-old Joseph Lapp stood in his front yard and fell to his knees as the dog slid into his warm embrace.

"I missed you." The boy dropped his head to Bailey's neck and scratched his back.

"Joseph, you must help your mother," Isaac said as he walked toward Tyler.

The boy waved goodbye and hurried back to the house.

"Welcome home." Tyler stretched out his hand. "How was your trip?"

The farmer looked tan and relaxed. "*Gut*. But I have twice the work to do now."

Tyler chuckled. "I know the feeling." He pointed to the coop in the backyard. "Eli Plank has been feeding the chickens. Thanks for arranging for his help."

Isaac smiled. "Eli is a fine boy and a hard worker."

Carrie stepped from the house and approached, smiling. "You must be Isaac Lapp." She introduced herself and shook hands with the tall Amish man. "You were visiting family?"

"We went to Florida. Some of my wife's family met us there."

"What part of Florida?"

"Pinecraft. It is an area that adjoins the city of Sarasota."

"On the Gulf Coast," Carrie said. "I usually go to Daytona or Cocoa Beach on the Atlantic side."

Ruth came from the house. Isaac motioned her forward and introduced her to Carrie. "Our son, Joseph." He pointed to the young boy standing near his mother. Bailey took a tennis ball to the boy, who threw it into the backyard.

Carrie laughed. "It seems that Bailey's missed you."

"Joseph has missed the dog even more," Ruth said with a knowing nod. "After your father was gone, the house was dark and lonely. We are sorry for what happened, but we are glad to see the house is open again."

"You've been traveling all day?"

"On a charter bus." Ruth gazed at the countryside and inhaled deeply. "The fresh air of home is good."

"It's dinnertime. I'm sure you're hungry. I made too many burgers, but it looks like the number is perfect if you join us?"

Ruth looked at her husband. "We were going to have some cheese and bread, Isaac. The meat would be nice after the trip."

He nodded to Carrie. "You are generous. *Denki*, but we have work to do. The bread and cheese will satisfy us till morning."

"The meat will take about thirty minutes to grill," Carrie insisted. "We can bring the burgers to you when they're done. If you don't have time to eat with us, at least you could share the food so it doesn't go to waste."

Ruth watched for her husband's reaction. He hesitated for a long moment and then nodded. "*Yah, Gott* would not want us to be wasteful."

"Thank you for your generosity," Ruth said as she

turned to follow her husband back to their house. "Joseph, you may play with Bailey until dinner is ready."

After they had taken the extra burgers to the Lapps and had dinner themselves, Carrie and Tyler stepped onto the front porch. "The stillness is comforting," she said as her gaze took in the surrounding farmland.

Turning, Tyler glanced at the old freestanding kitchen hugging the main house as well as the barn and the chicken coop. Even the field behind the house where he'd viewed Corporal Fellows's body seemed peaceful tonight. Was he being lulled into believing everything would be all right?

"It's late, Carrie. You need to get some sleep. Thanks again for inviting me to join you for dinner."

She smiled. "We'll do it again."

"Good." He hesitated a long moment and looked down into her pretty blue eyes, the color of the sky on a summer's day. A breeze stirred her hair, and the light scent of gardenias wafted past him. As much as he wanted to touch her cheek and feel the smoothness of her skin, he kept his hands at his sides and willed himself to step away.

"I'll see you tomorrow." A heaviness settled in his heart. What was wrong with him? He was thinking foolish thoughts that could ruin their somewhat strained relationship. There was no room for romance when a killer was on the loose.

He walked back to his house, thinking of the openness of her expression and how much he had wanted to draw her into his arms.

EIGHT

Carrie sat on the edge of the bed, exhausted. Before turning out the light, she checked Tyler's number on her phone, relieved that she could call him if she needed help.

Bailey whined and pranced around the room. She beckoned him closer and patted his head. "Is something wrong?"

Glancing out the window, she saw the chicken coop, the barn and the old kitchen house. The moon peered through the cloud cover and cast its glow over the field where the soldier's body had been found.

The memory of what she had seen played through her mind. Needing to push away the too-graphic thoughts, she headed for the bathroom and drew water into a glass, then drank it down. Padding into the second guest room, she eased back the curtain and peered out the other side of the house, seeing Tyler's ranch next door. A light glowed in one of the windows. Was he working late? Or staying awake to protect her?

She dropped the curtain back in place and returned to her bed. Bailey settled on the floor nearby. Eventually, Carrie drifted into a fitful sleep.

Again the memory of finding the body returned, only

this time she raced after Bailey toward the mound of a digital-patterned uniform. Circling the victim, she looked down and screamed. The soldier wasn't the man she'd found but Tyler.

Her eyes jerked open. She gasped for air. Looking around the room, she tried to get her bearings.

Sitting up, she wiped her hand over her eyes and shook her head to detach herself from the horrific dream. Dropping to her feet, she inhaled.

A chill tangled along her spine.

Smoke.

Bailey?

Standing, she glanced out the window.

Terror gripped her heart.

Fire!

The kitchen house was engulfed in flames.

Grabbing her phone, she screamed for Bailey, slipped on her robe and ran to the stairs. Taking them two at a time, she stumbled down the stairs, almost falling. Bailey stood at the door, barking.

She hit the speed dial for Tyler. The call went to voice mail. Where was he?

She disconnected, her fingers stiff, unyielding. The smoke drifted into the house. She coughed. Hit his number again.

"Please," she moaned. "I need help.

The phone rang in her ear. She threw open the front door and raced into the night.

Flames shot from the freestanding kitchen and licked the top rafter of the second story of the main house. The bedroom where she had slept just minutes before would quickly be engulfed in flames.

The house.

Her father's house.

"Carrie!" Tyler's voice came from the phone. "What's wrong?"

"Fire. Help me, Tyler."

"Fire, fire, fire."

Carrie screamed in the night as Tyler raced across the yard. She was too close, holding the garden hose and trying to put out the blaze with a mere trickle of water.

"Get back," he warned, pulling her away from the dancing flames.

A door slammed. Isaac ran to the bell behind his house. He tugged on the rope. The toll of the bell sounded in the night over the crackling fire.

"The men will come." Isaac grabbed buckets from his barn and pulled water from the well.

Just as he had promised, men ran from the neighboring houses and raced to the Harris home.

Tyler called 911. "Fire on Amish Road." He gave the address. "Tell the fire chief to hurry."

Eli Plank and his father, Simon, ran from across the street. They grabbed buckets and tossed water on the blaze. Other Amish men joined them and formed a bucket brigade, dousing the kitchen house.

Tyler looked at the hose. "It's been cut," he told Carrie as he turned off the spigot. "Find duct tape. In the barn."

She disappeared into the building and returned carrying a silver roll. Tyler wrapped it around the split hose. Not the best repair but good enough to feed water through.

He turned on the faucet. Water poured from the nozzle. Tyler wet down the side of the main house. A portion of the wood had blackened from the lick of flames, but the house hadn't caught.

He glanced at the bedroom above, knowing too well how close the fire had come.

More men filled the gaps, even some of the women, all helping.

Sirens screeched in the night; two fire trucks pulled into the driveway. Firemen dressed in turnout gear quickly attached their hoses and poured water onto the flames.

Once the fire was under control, Tyler glanced around for Carrie and found her standing with eyes wide. "He wanted to burn down the house," she said, her voice no more than a whisper. "He wanted to trap me inside."

She was right.

The attacks had turned violent. Someone didn't just want her to leave the area. He wanted her dead.

Carrie sat on the front steps and watched the firemen roll up their hoses and carry them back to their truck. Although her heart was heavy about the damage to the kitchen house, she was grateful for all those who had worked to save at least a portion of the structure. The huge fireplace, hearth and one of the two adjoining walls were still intact. When rebuilt, the structure would still maintain its historical significance, which was a relief, but she was most thankful that the main house had been saved.

Bailey lay at her feet and watched the firemen.

His tail wagged as Ruth Lapp approached carrying a sleepy Joseph in her arms.

Carrie smiled at the sweet boy. "Did the noise wake you?"

He nodded and wiggled free from his mother's hold. She placed the boy on the porch step and watched as he wrapped his arms around Bailey's neck.

"Joseph was awake and worried," Ruth said. "He feared Bailey had been hurt in the fire."

"They're fast friends."

"*Yah*. He would like a dog, but Isaac is not interested in having an animal in the house."

The little boy looked up with big eyes. "I told *Datt* I would take care of the dog."

"I know, Joseph, but your father knows what's best."

"I talked to *Gott*. He said a dog would be good for the family."

Ruth smiled. "You hear your own mind, Joseph."

"No, *Mamm*. I hear His voice."

Ruth turned as her husband approached.

"The fire is out, but I will watch tonight," Isaac said. "We do not want sparks to start anew."

Carrie stood. "Thank you, Isaac, and please thank our other neighbors. If it hadn't been for your help and theirs, the main house would have caught fire." She let out a ragged breath as she gazed up at the Harris home. "I can't imagine what would have happened."

"The house would have been quickly engulfed," one of the firemen chimed in as he approached. He nodded to Isaac. "Appreciate the help, Mr. Lapp. The water cooled everything down and kept the flames from spreading."

Tyler and the fire chief neared.

"Looks like it was a set fire, ma'am," the chief told Carrie. "A trail of accelerant led partially toward the house. The arsonist may have been interrupted."

"Bailey started barking, which must have scared him away. I looked outside as soon as I woke but didn't see anything at first. Then the flames caught." She glanced at Tyler. "That's when I called you."

"I'm sorry, Carrie." Tyler's face reflected the regret she heard in his voice. "I was talking to Everett and didn't realize you had phoned."

"Ruth heard Carrie's screams and woke me," Isaac interjected. "I saw no one. Only the fire."

"I'll bring the fire marshal out this way tomorrow," the chief said. "If you give me your cell number, Ms. York, I'll call you ahead of time to make sure you're home."

"That might be a problem," Carrie said. "I'm going to town in the morning to meet with my lawyer."

"Not to worry. We don't need to go inside the main house. I just wanted you to know I'd be on the property in case you came home to find two strange men prowling around your backyard."

The fire chief didn't realize the significance of his comment.

"Sir." One of the firemen hurried toward the chief. "We checked the chimney and fireplace in the old kitchen house and found a loose brick."

He glanced at Carrie. "When we tried to replace the brick, we found a small journal that looks old."

Carrie took the leather-bound book from the fireman's outstretched hand. He raised a flashlight and pointed to the page where a fragment of ribbon marked the spot.

"The book fell open as we pulled it free. A few of the guys and I couldn't help but notice the script," he told her. "You don't see writing like that these days. From the looks of the brittle pages, the journal has to be old."

Another fireman stood nearby. "Guess we were caught up in the moment, ma'am, and read a bit of the script.

The page we saw mentions buried treasure and actually tells where it's located."

Tyler looked over Carrie's shoulder and read from the journal, "...turn at the twisted oak and walk toward the row of blackberry bushes..."

Isaac rubbed his beard. "I'm not aware of a twisted oak."

Tyler nodded in agreement. "The tree's probably long gone."

Carrie turned the page. "There's more."

"You might want to check your property," one of the firemen suggested. "Most folks believe gold is buried around here."

Joseph pulled on his mother's skirt. "What if someone found the treasure, *Mamm*?"

"They would give it to Carrie, Joseph. This land is hers now."

She smiled at Ruth. "I still consider it my father's property."

Tyler's face darkened. No doubt he realized she was distancing herself from the land and the confusion that continued to haunt her. If she got rid of the property and the house, would she be able to leave the memory of her father here in Georgia when she returned to Washington?

Ruth stood and nudged her son. "I must get you home, Joseph."

The boy hugged Bailey and then placed his small hand in his mother's. *"Guten nacht,"* he said with a wave of his hand.

"Guten nacht," Carrie repeated back to him.

As she watched Joseph and his mother walk toward their house, Carrie sighed. Contrary to what she had wished the boy, the night wasn't good, because an evil person had struck again. Carrie had been saved from harm, but would there be a next time, and if so, would she escape alive?

Tyler helped the firemen load equipment onto their trucks and raised his hand in farewell as they pulled out of the driveway. Then he joined Carrie, who'd been watching from the porch.

Isaac stepped closer once the fire engines had turned onto Amish Road, heading back to their station. "I will check the kitchen house to make sure it is as the firemen said."

"Thank you, Isaac." Carrie smiled. "And again, thank you for coming to my aid."

"Neighbors help neighbors. The fire could have destroyed your house and mine. Fire is always a concern. *Gott* woke you in time."

Tyler felt the warm grasp of the farmer's friendship as they shook hands. "Thank you, neighbor."

"*Yah*, we are that."

Isaac nodded his farewell and walked toward what was left of the kitchen house.

Tyler turned to Carrie. "I'm sorry that I didn't answer your initial call for help."

"You couldn't have known."

"But I told you I'd be there for you."

"And you were, Tyler, although I'm concerned because the attacks are escalating. He wants to scare me away, yet I'm determined to stand my ground, at least until I decide what to do with the house."

"Maybe you should move to a hotel in town," Tyler suggested.

"No." She shook her head. "I'm staying here, in my

father's house. He won't strike again. At least not tonight. Plus, knowing you're next door is reassuring."

She turned toward the door. "I should go inside, although I don't think I'll be able to sleep."

He pointed to the aged journal she still held in her hand. "You could read yourself to sleep."

She smiled and raised the small leather-bound book. "Catching up on family history sounds like a good idea."

"How soon do you plan to return to DC?"

"I'm not sure. I'll know more after I talk to George Gates. What time did you want to go to town tomorrow?"

"How does nine o'clock sound?"

"Fine. I'll call the garage in the morning. The new tire should be in. If nothing else needs to be worked on, I'll be able to get my car back. Then I can travel to town on my own."

"That may not be the best idea. You need to be careful."

She nodded. "I'm all too aware of the danger."

In the distance, Isaac climbed the steps to his porch and entered his house. A soft glow of an oil lamp lit the downstairs window, only to be extinguished a few minutes later.

"I'll walk around the house a few times during the night to check on things, Carrie, so don't worry if you hear someone outside. I want to ensure that the fire remains out and that no one tries to pull something like that again."

"How will I know it's you and not someone out to do me harm?"

"Call my cell, if you're worried. I'll answer."

"On the first ring?"

He raised his right hand to his chest. "Cross my heart."

From the look that washed over her face, he knew his words had touched a place deep inside her.

"My mother used to say that," Carrie shared, her voice low and melancholy. "The funny thing is that she was talking about how much she loved me and how much she believed that my father would have loved me if he had been alive."

She glanced down. "Only she wasn't telling me the truth, Tyler. She was telling me lies."

"From what I've seen, your father did love you. He kept the house and property so he could pass it on to his only child. That's love. Your mother may have had problems of her own, and your childhood wasn't what you would have wished it to be, but she loved you. Your father—in his own way—did, as well."

"I'm not sure." Carrie clutched the leather journal to her chest. "Maybe I'll find something in the pages of this old journal that rings true. At least now I belong to a family. That's something I never had before."

"You have ancestors and a history."

"I hope it's a good history, of good people of whom I can be proud."

"Your dad was a good man, Carrie. You can be proud of him."

"I hope you're right, Tyler." She hesitated for a long moment and stared into his eyes.

He saw vulnerability and a woman who wanted to find her place in the history of this family. First she had to open her heart to her father. From everything that Tyler had heard, the sergeant major was a dedicated soldier and an honorable man, but he'd made a mistake in not contacting his daughter. If only Carrie could find the reason the sergeant major had stayed out of her life. If she knew why, she might be able to see beyond her pain and forgive her father.

Then he thought of her boss, the senator, and realized some mistakes were too big to be forgiven.

After Carrie went inside, Tyler circled the house and checked the old kitchen outbuilding, all too aware of the nearness of the main house and the danger that could have trapped Carrie inside. Looking up, he saw light glowing in the bedroom window directly above the out-building. The black charred marks on the main structure were a chilling reminder of what had happened tonight.

Flicking his gaze to the surrounding woods, he listened and watched for anything more that could bring her harm. The investigation was important, but Carrie's safety was his top priority. Tyler had to ensure that no harm came to her. He couldn't let down his guard, not when her life depended on him.

NINE

Although tired, Carrie crawled into bed determined to read the journal the firemen had found. Her eyes quickly grew heavy as she held the book and tried to decipher the writing. The script, although beautiful, was difficult to read, with its fluid swirls and flowering prose that people used in days long past.

The diary belonged to a young woman who longed for her husband's return from war. She had children at home, Anna and Benjamin, and an older son fighting alongside his father.

Carrie woke the next morning with the book still in her hands. She placed it on the nightstand, planning to read more after she returned from town. Quickly she dressed and headed to the kitchen for coffee.

Her cell chirped. Checking the caller ID, she saw her office number and answered the call. The senator's senior adviser's deep voice clipped a curt greeting. "We haven't heard from you, Carrie. I thought you were returning within forty-eight hours."

"It's taking me a bit longer to decide what to do with the property, Art."

"Sell. You don't want to be tied to some backroads area of Georgia."

"It's beautiful here."

"Maybe, but don't get sidelined by pretty countryside. You're a city girl with a career you need to grow. The senator is waiting for that speech."

"I told you I'd have it ready in the next day or two. Senator Kingsley usually doesn't look at his speeches until a few days before each event."

"This one is important. He wants more emphasis on cutting the military budget."

"I doubt that's a good idea at this time with the threats to national security coming out of the Middle East."

"Are you doubting the senator?"

She bristled. "Of course not. I'm just wondering if you have the right take on what he said."

"I heard him, Carrie, and I know what he wants, but if you insist on talking to him—"

"That might be a good idea."

Art sighed. "You know his busy schedule. He doesn't have time for you today."

"Then why did you mention it?" Frustrated, she paused for a moment before asking, "Are you sure he can't squeeze in a phone call?"

"I'm sure."

"I'll write the speech. Then maybe he'll have time to talk to me."

Hot tears burned her eyes as she disconnected. Art Adams wasn't speaking for Senator Kingsley, she felt sure. The senator was usually concerned about her well-being. She had expected him to call and find out personally how she was doing, especially if the staff had told him about the murder on her father's property.

They must not have informed him.

Unwilling to accept what Art said, she dialed the senator's private number and left a voice mail. "Senator Kingsley, I wanted you to know that things are going a little badly here in Georgia. I told you I didn't know my father, and now I'm trying to sort through what is true and what is not. You can understand the difficulty. I'm working on the speech, but I'd like to clarify a few points. Art said you wanted to emphasize the need for additional budget cuts for the military, but I'm not sure if that's what you really want or if that's Art's interpretation. Let me know, sir. I'd like to hear it from you."

She hung up feeling better and hurried into the kitchen. Hopefully she hadn't seemed needy, which was something she never wanted to be. She'd grown up with a mother who needed so much more than Carrie had been able to provide—support and love and affirmation. Whatever she did to help her mother, it had never been enough.

The sense of unworthiness she had felt as a child still resonated in her spirit, especially at times like this when she was enmeshed in the memories.

Determined to be strong, Carrie pulled bread from the wrapper and stuck it in the toaster, appreciating the high-end appliances in the newly remodeled kitchen. Had her father prepared the house for her? Or had he been getting it ready to sell as Gates had mentioned?

She put her head in her hands. If only she knew what to do and what would be the best for her own future and for this house.

In a strange way, she was beginning to see the man who had lived here. His books, his Bible, the devotionals and plaques with inspirational sayings that decorated his house. She had hoped to find a picture of herself. If only.

They'd never met, or at least she didn't think they had ever met. How could he have turned his back so completely on his own child when he had no one else? Especially since he seemed to have a relationship with the Lord. Could a godly man disavow his daughter?

He left you his estate.

The inner voice chastised her, yet she didn't want her father's house or his land. She wanted to know him, to have a relationship with a real person and not the memory, which wasn't even that. How could she have a memory when she didn't know him?

The toaster buzzed, but when the slice of bread popped up, the outside was too dark.

Was that her father's preference? She opened the cabinet seeing the rich roast coffee. No sugar. No fancy creamers. No tea or hot cocoa.

His refrigerator held hot sauce and pickles and horseradish mustard and a half-empty jar of yellow peppers.

Spicy food. Black coffee. No frills. No fuss. Was that her father?

She threw the toast in the trash and poured coffee into a mug, adding a heavy dollop of half-and-half she'd bought at the grocery and a rounded teaspoon of sugar. Evidently she hadn't followed her father's taste in coffee. Lifting the mug to her lips, she inhaled the rich aromas and sipped the hearty brew.

Mmm. Good. Not the mild roast she was used to. Maybe her father could teach her a thing or two after all.

She almost smiled.

Glancing out the window, she raked her fingers through her hair and straightened her blouse when Tyler stepped outside and glanced her way. Surely he couldn't see her through the window. She took a step back and peered ever so carefully over her mug, watching as he stretched.

Dressed in athletic shorts and an army T-shirt, he looked muscular and tall, and a curl of interest twisted through her insides that was mildly disconcerting. She didn't need to notice anything of interest in the special agent. He was investigating the soldier's death and was a neighbor. Nothing more, she told herself as she tried to glance away.

Her eyes returned to watch Tyler jog out of his driveway and along Amish Road. In the distance, she spied the Plank Farm. A man wearing a dark hat waved as Tyler passed.

Weren't the Amish usually standoffish? Perhaps the recent danger had brought them all together. Either that or they'd had—as Tyler had mentioned yesterday—a good relationship with her father that carried over.

She pulled a second slice of bread from the wrapper, stuck it in the toaster and turned down the timer. The result was light brown toast, the way she liked it.

Opening the fridge, she pulled out a stick of butter and strawberry jelly that appeared to be homemade. The seal on the top of the jar was from the Amish Craft Shoppe. She'd have to ask Ruth about the store, imagining the fresh vegetables and baked goods she might find there.

Tyler returned soon after she had eaten the toast and finished her coffee. She stuck the mug and plate in the dishwasher and again paused to watch him stretch to cool down.

Even from this distance she could see the ruddy hue to his flushed skin and his tussled hair. In spite of his workout gear, he looked exceedingly attractive.

Maybe there was a less formal, less by-the-book side

of him. If only he would let down some of his guard at times so she could feel more at ease around him.

After wiping the counter clean, she ran upstairs to put on makeup and comb her hair. Returning to the main floor, she let Bailey out to run and waited on the front porch until he bounded back to her.

Joseph tumbled out of his house as if he'd been waiting for the dog. The two met in the grassy area between the homes.

"I'm going into town for a bit, Joseph. If you want to play ball with Bailey, I know he'd enjoy the exercise before he has to go back inside."

She tossed the boy the ball, and the two frolicked in the yard. Bailey's barks mixed with Joseph's laugher and brought a sense of well-being to her heart.

If only coming to Freemont could have been different.

The sound of footsteps caused her to turn. Tyler walked toward her, dressed in a crisp cotton shirt and navy slacks. The blue windbreaker had CID on the left breast, reminding her that there was an ongoing investigation.

"Looks like Bailey's getting lots of good exercise," he said with a smile as he watched Joseph and the dog.

"Joseph said he wants a dog, and God told him he'd get one, but evidently Isaac isn't interested."

Tyler laughed. "I have a feeling Joseph might be able to change his father's mind."

"I…I don't know what I'll do with Bailey when I sell the property."

Tyler glanced at her. "So you're putting the house on the market?"

She shook her head. "I don't know."

"You've got a career to go back to, Carrie. I'm sure

you worked hard to get where you are, and while I don't have anything good to say about the man you work for, landing a speechwriting position in DC is to be admired."

"I don't understand your feelings about the senator. You've just heard things through the news. You don't know him. If you'd met him, you'd have a different opinion."

"No, Carrie." Tyler shook his head. "Nothing can change my mind about Drake Kingsley."

She bristled, unable to understand such a one-sided viewpoint. That was Tyler's problem—he formed opinions that didn't necessarily bear out. If only he could soften a bit and see the way things really were.

"I'll get my coat." Turning back to the house, she realized she didn't see clearly either. No matter what people said about her father, she couldn't believe he was a good man.

Maybe she and Tyler had that in common. Two controlling people who held on to their beliefs too tightly.

"Bailey, it's time to come inside."

The dog wagged his tail and waited as Joseph patted his ears; then, holding the tennis ball in his mouth, Bailey raced into the house.

"I won't be gone long," she told the dog as she grabbed her purse and coat. Stepping outside, she closed and locked the door behind her.

Another day to learn more about her father. Another day with Tyler Zimmerman, a man who focused on facts and evidence instead of people.

She didn't belong here. She belonged back in Washington, DC.

Or did she?

* * *

Tyler remained quiet as he drove Carrie into town. He didn't want to talk about the senator and the man who had changed his past and not for the better.

She wouldn't understand. Carrie was focused on the senator as a boss and maybe an older man who stood in a father's place. She was mistaken. Royally wrong, but she needed to learn the truth about him by herself.

Hopefully she wouldn't be hurt from her mistaken allegiance to someone who wasn't worth her praise or adulation. If only she could have seen the man Kingsley had been years earlier.

The memory of what had happened that fateful night still burned within Tyler.

"Did you want to go to the lawyer's office first?" he asked, needing to focus on the present instead of the past.

She nodded. "If you don't mind. I want to talk to George about my father's land. He said there was a buyer and that my father was interested in selling."

"Didn't his receptionist say that your father had changed his mind?"

"She could have been confused, Tyler."

"Maybe, but I wonder if Gates was seeing things through his own financial gain."

"Meaning what?" Carrie asked.

"Meaning he wanted to negotiate the sale and earn a nice paycheck. He may be thinking of his own pocketbook instead of what would be the best for you and the property."

"Then I'll ask for the buyer's name and contact the person myself," she insisted.

"Flo mentioned a corporation that was interested in

the land, Carrie. When a big buyer is on the horizon, everyone wants to get into the action. That could be a problem."

She drew her hand protectively to her neck. "Surely you don't think someone in the corporation is attacking me."

"More likely it's a local person who sees himself as a middleman and wants you out of the picture."

"Are you accusing George Gates?"

"I'm not accusing anyone, but I'm being truthful, Carrie. Someone's out to do you harm."

"Which I'm well aware of," she said. "It's just that I'm not sure who's on my side."

"I'm on your side, and I'm here because I'm concerned about your safety."

"That's not totally true, Tyler. You're here because you were assigned to watch me as part of the investigation."

"I'm assigned to ensure that you aren't harmed." He saw a flash of confusion in her pretty eyes. "I won't let anything happen to you, Carrie."

She pulled in a ragged breath and shook her head. "I'm sorry if I sound antagonistic, but I'm worried and confused, and I don't know who I can trust."

"You can trust me, Carrie."

She stared at him for a long moment. "I…I hope I can."

He gripped the steering wheel tightly, frustrated that she questioned his desire to keep her safe. If only she would open up and share more with him, but she remained closed and reserved.

He pulled into the Gates Law Firm parking lot and killed the engine. Carrie was out of the car before he could open her door.

"Did you want company when you talk to Gates?"

She shook her head. "I'll go in alone."

"You're sure?"

She nodded and headed for the back door. Tyler glanced around the lot, realizing too quickly that he didn't want to wait outside. He followed Carrie into the building and nodded to the receptionist.

Flo was equally as made-up as she had been the day prior and smiled widely as they entered.

She pointed to George Gates's office. "You can go in, Ms. York. Mr. Gates is expecting you."

Carrie glanced at Tyler over her shoulder. "This won't take long." She opened the door to the lawyer's personal office and closed it behind her.

Tyler smiled at Flo and then glanced at the people sitting in the adjoining waiting room. "Busy place."

She batted her eyes. "Mr. Gates has a lot of clients."

"There was a soldier here yesterday. Jason Jones. He works for the chaplain on post."

Flo nodded. "Jason's my nephew."

"Really?" Tyler hadn't expected the connection.

"He stops by to see me when he comes to town." She closed a manila folder on her desk before asking, "Did you visit the museum?"

Tyler nodded. "Thanks for telling us about the displays."

"You saw the items the sergeant major had donated?"

"And the other memorabilia, as well."

"What about the letter written by Jefferson Harris? The hint of buried treasure always gets folks' attention."

"I'm sure it does," Tyler agreed. "I was struck by Jefferson's love of family and home. I'd hate to see the Harris property go to someone who didn't appreciate the family history."

Tyler paused before adding, "You mentioned that a corporation from out of town was interested in buying the land. Do you have any additional information?"

"Not about the corporation, but there's been talk that the mayor's wife wanted to turn the house into a B and B. In fact, Mrs. Gates said she wouldn't mind doing the same. The property has a lot of potential."

"I'm sure. There's enough acreage to build some houses too."

Flo lowered her voice. "A mall is what I heard."

The receptionist's comment took him by surprise. "A shopping mall?"

"But with an Amish theme. Craft shops, small restaurants, a grocery mart that sells Amish items."

"Do you know the name of the corporation?"

"No." Flo shook her head. "I don't have a name, and I've probably said too much."

Tyler held up his hand. "Nonsense. You've just been neighborly. I've enjoyed learning some of the local news."

The receptionist smiled as if pleased by his comments. "That's prime real estate if you ask me. Anyone would love to buy the land. Folks are interested in Amish areas now. A resort, a hotel or boutique shops catering to tourists would do well there."

"I doubt the Amish would be happy."

The phone rang.

"Perhaps not." She lifted the receiver.

The door to the lawyer's office opened. George Gates stood in the doorway.

Tyler moved closer. "If you've got a minute, sir, I'd like to talk to you along with Ms. York."

Gates glanced at his watch as if to make an excuse.

Ignoring the lawyer's attempt to shove him aside, Tyler

looked at Carrie. "We need to discuss the buyers who are interested in your father's property."

"George mentioned a large construction company had talked to my father," Carrie explained. "He was initially interested but then declined the offer."

"Were there other offers?" Tyler looked at the lawyer.

Gates splayed his fingers. "As I told Carrie, I'm sure a number of local people would be interested in acquiring the property. The home is lovely and has been well maintained. The acreage provides a lovely setting in the midst of the Amish area. Perfect for folks who want a quiet environment to raise their families."

"Or change the home into a bed-and-breakfast," Tyler countered.

"I'm not following you," the lawyer said.

"Isn't that why the mayor's wife wants to buy the land?"

"She's expressed some interest," Gates admitted, "but I'm not sure that's what Carrie wants."

She shook her head. "I don't want a business venture to disturb the Amish way of life."

"What about a shopping center?" Tyler threw out.

Gates wrinkled his brow. "You're imagining things."

"Am I? Isn't that what some folks are interested in doing?"

"I would never agree to that," Carrie said. "Anything that would bring more traffic to the area would hurt the Amish neighbors, who have been so helpful to me."

She looked at Tyler. "I told George about the fire last night."

"Any idea," Tyler asked, "who might want to burn down the historic home? The fire chief claimed it was arson."

Gates tugged on his chin. "Have you found anything more about the soldier who was murdered? Perhaps military personnel are involved."

A stab at Tyler for sure. "The investigation is ongoing. Let me know if you hear anything from the townspeople or anyone else who is interested or disgruntled because Ms. York doesn't want to sell the property."

"But she is interested." George smiled at Carrie. "You need to inform the special agent about your plans."

Tyler was confused. He looked at Carrie. "You're planning to sell?"

She tilted her head. "At this point, I'm just gathering information."

"Someone's trying to get you to leave town, Carrie. You said yourself that if you do so, they've won. That's not what your father would want."

"Right now I'm not sure of anything involving my father. What he wants is not my concern, Tyler. I have to determine what's best for me."

"And the Amish neighbors?"

"Of course, I'll take their needs into consideration, as well."

Tyler glanced at the lawyer. "Thanks for your time." He opened the rear door and held it for Carrie, who said goodbye and then hurried to the parking lot.

"I don't know why you sound angry," she said once they had settled into Tyler's car.

"I don't like that guy. He seems to know more than he's letting on. From the way it looks, he's probably going to make a nice profit from the sale of your father's property. We'll know more once he tells you the names of all those interested."

"There's got to be more involved than just the land."

"Add buried treasure to the mix, Carrie, and you have a good motive for murder."

"Corporal Fellows or my father?"

"Maybe both."

TEN

Carrie couldn't understand Tyler's bad mood. Maybe he was upset because he hadn't been able to solve Corporal Fellows's murder.

"Have you heard anything more from the local police?" she asked.

"Not this morning. Let's stop at the garage first and check on your car. Then we can visit the police department. I'd like to talk to Phillips."

The garage wasn't far. Tyler pulled in front of the shop and killed the engine.

From the sign on the door, Earl Vogler, the mechanic on duty, was the owner, as well. The beefy man nodded as they stepped from the car. "Be with you folks in a minute."

He turned back to the attractive woman in stiletto heels, a low-cut top and a skimpy skirt with whom he had been previously talking. From the sour look on her face, she was evidently upset.

Earl shrugged his broad shoulders. "I can work on your car first thing tomorrow morning, ma'am, but not before."

She pursed her lips. "That's ridiculous."

"Actually it's because the part is still in Atlanta and won't arrive until close of business today."

"Then work late."

"Ma'am, my grandsons are playing ball tonight. I want to watch their games."

"If that's the case, I'll be forced to spread word around town that you're not a good mechanic."

He sighed with frustration. "Mrs. Gates, my garage is the best in town, but you can go to my competition, if you so choose. They won't be able to get the part any faster than I can."

She huffed. "Then I'll bring my car back in the morning. You can work on it then."

"I open at seven-thirty."

"I'll be here at nine-thirty, after my aerobics class at the gym."

"It's first come, first serve. I can't guarantee my workload by that point, ma'am. It might be afternoon before your car will be ready."

She let out a lungful of frustration. "Tomorrow morning then at seven-thirty. I may have my husband drop the car off. You know George Gates, don't you?"

"Can't say that I've met Mr. Gates."

"Of Gates Law Firm."

"I'll look forward to meeting him tomorrow."

She hurried to her car and peeled out of the parking lot, no doubt still frustrated.

The mechanic shook his head as he approached Tyler and Carrie. "Takes all kinds."

"That was George Gates's wife?" Carrie asked the man.

"You know him?"

"He was my father's lawyer."

"Gates does a good job from what I've heard, but his wife thinks she's entitled to special privileges." He sighed. "Might save me a lot of headaches if she takes her business elsewhere. I have a feeling she'll never be satisfied with the work I do."

He shook his head regretfully. "'Course you're here about your own car. I looked it over yesterday. It's good to go except for needing a new tire. My distributor is trying to find a match with your other three. Soon as the new one comes in, I'll put it on and have the car ready for you. Might be tomorrow or the day following."

Carrie looked at Tyler. "Which means I'll have to beg more rides from you."

"Not a problem." Glancing back at the mechanic, he said, "I heard Mrs. Gates runs a home design business."

The mechanic nodded. "She calls it a boutique. Real pricey stuff from what folks have told me. She takes old homes and restores them, then decorates them with the high-end furnishing from her business."

"I'm surprised she has many customers in a small town like this," Tyler said.

The mechanic smiled. "Don't let Freemont's size fool you. We're got some industry here. The fort brings in a lot of folks, as well. Military retire in the local area. Some of them start their own businesses. The moneyed folks live in the country club community. Big homes with even bigger price tags. Too pricey for my budget."

"What about the mayor and his wife? Do they live there?"

"They have a house in town, but she works in Mrs. Gates's boutique. There's talk they might start flipping homes on the side."

"Who would do their demo and reconstruction work?"

"Sorry, I don't have a clue. The wife and I moved in with her mother after we married. We've never had to buy a house." He nodded to Carrie. "I'll call you when that tire comes in."

"An interesting mix of folks," Tyler said as they returned to his car. "And they all have something to gain by acquiring your father's property."

"Now I understand why Gates encouraged me to sell. His wife wants to buy the property."

"Which means he's not providing sound advice about your father's estate. Let's stop by police headquarters and talk to Phillips. He'll be interested in what we've learned."

Tyler drove to the Freemont Police Department, hoping they had uncovered more information that could end the case and bring the guilty to justice. If only the information they'd learned at the garage would fit somehow into the mix, or at least provide clues as to who was attacking Carrie.

The CID had researched Corporal Fellows's background and found a low-key guy without much history. He had gotten in trouble with a superior once during basic training, but since then he'd kept his nose clean.

Why he had rented a trailer at the sergeant major's property was the question Tyler kept asking. Did he have anything to do with the sergeant major's so-called accidental death?

Officer Inman had taken the day off, but Phillips ushered them into his cubicle and invited them to sit down and have a cup of coffee. The brew was hearty, and both Tyler and Carrie were eager to share what they had found about Mrs. Gates's home design business.

Phillips listened to the information and nodded when Tyler finished talking. "Mrs. Gates's business is out of my range, for sure, and anyone here in the PD, but she's attracted folks from as far away as Macon and Columbus."

"Do you find it strange that she's interested in the Harris property when her husband is handling the estate?"

Phillips took a swig of his coffee, then set the cup on his desk. "Nothing wrong with Mrs. Gates running the business or wanting to buy the property. I don't like her husband being secretive about the interested buyer, but that would eventually come to light when the property went to sale. Unless, of course, he used a corporation name, and Mrs. Gates didn't come to the signing."

Carrie sighed. "Meaning he'd keep me in the dark or tell me it was an out-of-town venture, which is evidently what my father thought."

"I'm not saying there wasn't an interested buyer from outside the area," the cop added. "But Gates certainly has a vested interest in his wife buying the property."

"Do you know about any construction team that might work for her?"

"Nelson Quinn is a local real estate agent. He's flipped a few houses on the side. I heard he sometimes works with Mrs. Gates."

"So we've got a real estate agent, a designer who stages the homes for sale and a lawyer who handles the paperwork and ensures that every *i* is dotted and *t* is crossed." Tyler ticked off the various people involved on his fingers. "Looks like Gates and his wife have a nice business going."

"Which is perfectly legal," the officer pointed out.

Carrie tilted her head. "But what if my father initially planned to sell and then changed his mind?"

"Which sounds like what happened," Tyler added.

Phillips rubbed his chin. "Again there's nothing illegal about him changing his mind."

"But," Carrie said, "what if his accidental death wasn't an accident?"

Phillips glanced at Tyler. "That puts a different slant on things."

Tyler leaned forward. "You mentioned that a teen found the sergeant major's body."

"That's right. An Amish kid." Phillips swiveled his chair to face his computer. He tapped the keyboard and pulled up a file on the monitor. "Here it is. The dispatcher got a 911 call from Matthew Schrock, age fifteen, who discovered the body in a wooded area. The boy had smelled something. Saw turkey vultures overhead and took a closer look."

"Where did he find a phone?"

"Probably the Amish Craft Shoppe. It's located at the northern corner of Amish Road. They've got a pay phone there. As you probably know, the Amish don't allow phones in their homes, but they sometimes have them in their barns to use them for business purposes. A couple of the dairy farmers sell their milk to larger dairies and communicate by cell phone. Also, they use them for emergencies."

"Anything else in the report?"

Phillips studied his computer screen. "The deceased appeared to have slipped down the hillside to his death. He had a lump on the right side of his head."

"Any sign that he'd been in a fight?"

"'Abrasions to his face and hands consistent with having fallen through the bramble' is what the report says."

"What about his clothing?"

"He was wearing a hunting vest, cargo trousers and a plaid fleece shirt. Hiking boots."

"A hunting vest? What did it contain?"

"Hmm?" Phillips pursed his lips as he read the online report. "Seven rounds of ammo in the pockets, .30-30 caliber."

"Anyone find a rifle?"

"The officer on-scene searched the surrounding area, but found nothing else. Emergency rescue retrieved the body and transported it to the morgue."

"Was an autopsy done?"

"It was. Cause of death was trauma to the head and a broken neck."

Carrie gasped. "A broken neck? Was the officer who retrieved the body convinced it was an accidental fall?"

"A good question that we need to answer." Phillips reached for his phone and tapped in a number. "See if Officer Wittier is available. Tell him I want to talk to him."

Disconnecting, he pushed back from his computer. "He's in the building. Ray's a good kid with an excellent record in law enforcement. I'm sure he was thorough in his search of the area."

Ray Wittier quickly arrived. He was tall and lean but with a softness to his features that made him look young and immature. Tyler guessed him to be midtwenties, although he could have passed for a teenager.

Phillips quickly filled him in on what they had already discussed.

"Did you give any thought to a possible homicide?" Carrie asked.

"No, ma'am. The injury to the body seemed consistent with a fall. That hill's steep. Lots of leaves. We'd been having rain, so they were slippery. Easy enough for a person, even someone used to wandering the trails in that area, to lose his footing and tumble down that hill. The autopsy revealed a broken neck."

"What about his hunting vest?" Tyler pointed to Phillips's computer. "The report said ammo was found in his pockets. Did you look for a weapon?"

"I did. I even walked to the top of the ridgeline from where he must have fallen. An area of leaves was disturbed. Looked like he slipped and tried to right himself, then lost his footing and toppled to his death."

"Did you see signs of a scuffle?"

The young cop thought for a moment. "In hindsight, that could have been the case, although I never thought of a struggle at the time."

"The Amish boy you talked to—"

"Matthew Schrock," Ray volunteered.

"What did he say?" Tyler asked.

"Only that he had been walking through the woods and smelled something that had died. He decided to investigate and saw the body."

"Did you ask him about a rifle?"

"No. But at the time, I didn't think there was any reason to ask the question."

"Did Matthew's father come with you when you retrieved the body?"

"Yes, sir, along with the teenager."

"Did the father give any indication that his boy might have held back information?"

Ray shook his head. "The Amish are hesitant to call in the police, but we've never had a problem with prevarication." He looked at Phillips. "Wouldn't you agree, sir?"

"That's right. They may not provide as much information as we'd sometimes like, but a lack of honesty is never something we worry about." Phillips stood. "Thanks for talking to us, Ray."

Tyler pointed to Carrie. "Ms. York wants to learn as much as she can about her father's death. I'm sure you can understand her concern, seeing how Sergeant Major Harris's death was so tragic."

"I am sorry for your loss, ma'am." Ray turned to Officer Phillips. "Let me know if you need anything else, sir."

"Will do, Ray. Thanks for your help."

Tyler stood once the younger officer left the room. "We'll talk to the Amish boy. Do you have an address for him?"

Phillips checked the computer. "It just says Amish Road. Want me to call Ray back?"

Tyler held up his hand. "We'll find the kid. You've done enough already."

Carrie stood, and they both shook hands with Officer Phillips before they left the headquarters and drove back to the Amish community.

"We're going to talk to Matthew?" she asked.

"Exactly. I want to hear what he saw and compare notes. Isaac and Ruth will surely know how to locate him, but the Amish Craft Shoppe isn't far from where we intersect Amish Road. If we turn north and ride a couple miles, we'll find it. Let's stop there."

Carrie smiled. "Might be a good time to get to know the shop owner. He may have known my father. Seems everyone did. I only wish someone could provide more information about his death. I can't see how a man who had deployed numerous times to the Middle East could trip and fall down a hill to his death."

Tyler had to agree. "A lot of people have a little piece

of the puzzle of his death. We need to keep searching for the various parts and then try to put them together."

"And Corporal Fellows's death?" Carrie asked. "Will that fit into the puzzle, as well?"

"We'll have to wait and see."

"I'm running out of time, Tyler."

"Because you're ready to go back to Washington?"

"Because I need to decide what to do about the land."

"Gates can't force you to make a decision if you're not ready," Tyler insisted.

"But Senator Kingsley needs me back in DC."

"You don't have to go, Carrie."

"I do, if I want to keep my job."

This was only an investigation, Tyler realized. As much as he wanted Carrie to stay on the property, she needed to return to her job, working for a man who had caused so much pain in Tyler's life. He had hoped Carrie would see the senator for who he truly was, but she saw what she wanted to see.

Unfortunately the senator was a sham. Her mother had created a fictional tale about her father, and Carrie had created her own fictional impression of the senator.

Both were wrong.

But he wouldn't tell Carrie about her mistake. She would have to find that out for herself, probably long after she left Freemont.

Tyler would have moved on to a new assignment by then, but he'd always remember the pretty speechwriter who had tugged at his heart.

ELEVEN

The Amish Craft Shoppe looked as if it had stepped out of the pages of time. Carrie smiled when she spied the wraparound porch, welcoming hand-painted sign over the door and the winter pansies that circled the front of the building. Tyler braked to a stop on the gravel lot in front of the small establishment, and they quickly entered.

Long, hand-hewn tables were covered with freshly baked breads, pies, cakes and cookies as well as jars of jam and vegetables. On the shelves behind the counter were bolts of fabric in subdued colors, no doubt in keeping with Amish rules of dress found in the *Ordnung*, the Amish guide as to how they were to live their lives. Felt hats for winter, straw for summer hung from a free-standing wire shelf, along with suspenders and sewing supplies.

Thick quilts stitched in intricate patterns were draped over racks. Others were neatly folded and piled on a side table. Farther along the wall were bins of potatoes, both golden and sweet, onions, bunches of carrots and turnips and other tubers.

A young Amish man stood near the counter with broom in hand. "*Gut* morning. May I help you?"

"I'm sure I'll find a number of things to buy." Carrie glanced at Tyler.

He stepped closer and held up his identification. "I'm with the Criminal Investigation Division at Fort Rickman. I'm looking for Matthew Schrock."

"Matthew sometimes works here but not today. Is there a problem?"

Tyler shook his head. "Nothing that reflects poorly on him. He found a body in the woods about two weeks ago, and I wanted to talk to him about what he saw."

"Mr. Harris." The clerk nodded, his face somber. "Everyone was so sorry to learn of his death."

"Did Matthew mention anything about calling the police?"

"I was here when he and his *Datt* came to the store to use the telephone. Matthew was emotional, naturally. Uncovering a dead body would be very upsetting."

"Do you know where we can find the boy?"

"You should find him at home."

Tyler nodded. "Could you direct us?"

The clerk raised his hand. "Along Amish Road. Turn south when you leave the parking lot."

"Is it far?"

"Three or four miles at most."

As Tyler talked, Carrie gathered potatoes, onions, a loaf of bread and an apple pie. She placed them on the counter.

"Did you find everything you wanted?" Tyler asked.

"I did. Plus some. From the amount I'm buying, it looks like I'm staying in Freemont longer than a day or two."

Tyler smiled. "If you buy too much, you can always invite a neighbor over for dinner."

She laughed. "That sounds like a good solution. Do you like apple pie?"

"Doesn't everyone?"

"My *Datt* prefers peach pie," the young man said, joining in the discussion.

"Shall I get a peach pie, as well?" Carrie asked. "I could take a pie to Ruth. They've been so nice, and I'm sure she's busy unpacking and washing clothes after their trip."

"I doubt Isaac or Joseph would object."

Carrie added a second pie to the counter and paid the clerk once he had totaled the bill. Tyler helped carry the food to the car and opened the door for her.

"Did you notice the beautiful quilts?" she asked as she slipped onto the passenger seat. "I'd love to take one back to DC with me."

A muscle in Tyler's jaw twitched, which she'd noticed every time she mentioned returning to DC. She wasn't sure what it meant, but his enthusiasm had waned and his expression had grown somber.

"Are you okay?" she asked.

"Of course. Let's drop the food off at your house before we talk to the Amish boy. It sounds as if his house isn't far from your dad's place."

"That's fine with me." She hesitated a moment before adding, "There's one thing that bothers me about leaving the area."

Tyler turned expectantly and stared at her. "What's that?"

"Leaving my Amish neighbors. Ruth is a lovely lady, and although I don't know Isaac well, he's a good man, and Joseph has stolen my heart. Such a sweet little boy."

"The Lapps are good folks, and Joseph is a cute little

boy." Tyler's muscle twitched again. "But what about the neighbor on the other side?"

Surprised by the question, Carrie didn't know what to say and laughed to cover up her mixed emotions.

"I'm blessed with good neighbors on each side," she finally added, hoping to deflect any more comments.

Tyler seemed focused on the investigation and nothing else, but perhaps she was wrong about him. Maybe there was something more to the special agent than solving crimes.

Tyler pulled into Carrie's drive and carried the produce and baked goods into the house.

"Shall I fix sandwiches?" she asked. "It's almost lunchtime, and I'm getting hungry."

"We should have stopped in town. I could have bought you lunch."

"That wasn't necessary." She opened the refrigerator. "Ham and cheese on wheat sound good?"

"Better than I'd have at home."

She pulled the meat and cheese from the refrigerator and placed them on the counter. "You're not a gourmet cook?" she teased.

"I can grill. Does that count?"

"Sure. Those burgers were delicious last night. A couple of them are left over, if you'd prefer that for lunch."

"Surprise me."

"Let's do the ham and cheese. If you want, we can have leftover burgers tonight."

"I'll need a rain check. I've got a meeting at CID headquarters. They often run longer than expected. I wouldn't want to hold you up."

"And I didn't mean to insert myself into your schedule."

"No, it's nothing like that."

But it probably was. Carrie had failed to consider that Tyler might have a special someone on post. Someone he saw on a regular basis. Next time, she would keep her ideas for a shared meal to herself.

She fixed the two sandwiches, added chips and a pickle and placed them on the small table near the window, along with two glasses of iced tea.

"Good view of my house." Tyler laughed as he sat down and glanced out the kitchen window.

"I hadn't noticed." Her cheeks burned.

He stared at her for a long moment before he reached for his sandwich.

"I don't usually say grace," she blurted out. "But being around the Amish and seeing my father's Bible, it seems right."

Tyler returned the sandwich to the plate. "My dad never let me eat without giving thanks to the Lord for the food, as well as for those who had prepared the meal. He often prayed that the food would do good and not harm us in any way."

"Sounds like your dad was a good man."

"He loved the Lord. As I got older, I realized he loved me, as well." He shrugged. "Raising a child alone is tough on guys."

She thought of her mother. "On women too."

"Sorry, of course, your mom raised you alone."

"But she wasn't God-fearing, and she didn't teach me to pray. I got it from an osmosis of sorts visiting friends who had more stable home lives. Sometimes I'd go to church with them, but never with my mother."

"I'm sorry."

"At the time, I didn't think I was so far out of the norm. Later, in college, I realized other moms weren't quite as neurotic as mine, nor did other moms have a need to constantly be the center of attention."

"You could never measure up to what she wanted?"

"Exactly." She bowed her head. "Father God, thank You for bringing me to Freemont and for all those who have lived in this house. Bless the farmers who grew the food we are about to eat and the people who prepared it for sale." She glanced at Tyler. "Let it be good for our bodies and do no harm."

"Amen." He bit into the sandwich and smiled. "Delicious."

"You're just hungry."

"I never lie."

She laughed. "That's a quality I admire."

"You haven't mentioned the journal."

"I was so tired last night that I didn't get much read. The journal belonged to a woman named Charlotte Harris, who lived during the Civil War. She loved her family, and she loved to write."

"Like you."

"Perhaps I inherited my appreciation for the written word from her. Charlotte had an older son fighting in the war along with her husband. A younger son and daughter lived at home with her."

"Any mention of treasure?"

"I started at the beginning so I haven't gotten to the page the fireman noticed. She wrote about hiding some of the family keepsakes, which is different from buried treasure. Plus, there was no mention of gold coins."

"But there could have been coins."

"Of course. I'm wondering if the letter we saw in the Freemont Museum was penned by her husband, perhaps before he went off to fight."

"Or he could have come home injured before the end of the war or before the Union forces headed into Georgia. The letter mentioned his concern about Northern aggression taking what rightfully belonged to his children."

Tyler reached for the second half of his sandwich. "Have you looked at any of your father's things? He may have a family tree tucked away with his papers."

"There's an office in the back of the house with French doors that lead outside. I thought it might have been a screened-in porch that someone turned into a sunroom. He has bookshelves and a beautiful antique rolltop desk."

"Have you found anything of interest there?"

She placed the rest of her sandwich on the plate and wiped her hands on the napkin in her lap. "I know it sounds foolish, but I haven't wanted to infringe on the private areas in the house."

"You haven't opened the desk?"

"Nor have I gone in his bedroom or through his papers. I'm living as if I were a guest in a home that rightfully belongs to me, or will when all the paperwork is completed."

"You're not ready to accept him as your father?"

"Maybe that's the problem, but it seems a bit foolish of me, since he is my father, whether I claim him or not."

"Are you hesitant to embrace your father because of some skewed allegiance you have to your mother?"

Carrie titled her head. "I never thought of that as being the problem, but perhaps you're right."

"The people were nice at the first foster home I went to after my father's death, but I wouldn't open myself to them for fear I was dishonoring my dad. No one could or would take his place. At least that's the way my childish logic worked. I was struggling with a lot of things— anger, guilt, grief. Eventually the family sent me back, saying I wasn't willing to accept them into my life. Which was true at the time. Only—"

She waited. "Only what, Tyler?"

"Only that was the best home foster care could offer me. The next people were a whole lot worse, which only made me even angrier. I was kicked from home to home because of who I was. Each place was a step down, and my hate escalated."

"Sounds as if you were on a slippery slope to self-destruction. How'd you turn that around?"

"A high school coach saw something in me. Plus, he needed a lineman for the football team. For whatever reason, I let him into my pain. He loved God and tried to get me to join his church. I never went that far, but I listened and some of it rubbed off on me. He encouraged me to join high school ROTC, and I found my spot. We worked with the local police, and for a number of reasons, law enforcement and the military drew my interest."

"Did you enlist after high school to join the CID?"

"First the military police. Then I got a degree in criminal justice, thanks to Uncle Sam, and applied to be in the CID. I wanted to investigate crime and injustice done against military personnel and their families."

"You're a success story."

"Maybe, but I still harbor a grudge against the past."

"At your father?"

"At the man who killed him."

Carrie looked puzzled. "I thought your dad lost his life in an auto accident."

"He did, but the man driving the car that killed him was drunk."

She reached out and touched Tyler's hand. "I'm so sorry."

"It happened long ago, but I still remember how the guy staggered from his car. He reeked of alcohol and slurred his speech when he asked me if I was okay."

"You were in the car?"

"Luckily in the backseat. My forehead was cut." He touched a small scar that was probably a constant reminder of what had happened.

"He went to jail?"

Tyler laughed ruefully. "If only the world were a perfect place."

"You mean he wasn't found guilty?"

"He wasn't even accused of wrongdoing, Carrie, because he was a man of influence who knew the right people."

"Is there anything you can do now?"

Tyler shook his head. "What's the Bible say about vengeance?"

"As I recall, something about *vengeance being mine, sayeth the Lord.*"

"I'm waiting for God to bring the guilty to justice in my father's case and working hard to help the Lord in the cases I can handle."

He reached again for his sandwich. Carrie took a sip of iced tea and tried to imagine what Tyler had gone through. She had thought her own childhood was hard, but it was nothing compared to his.

As soon as they finished eating, she cleared the table and both of them rinsed the dishes and placed them in the dishwasher.

Her phone rang, a local number she didn't recognize. "I should take this."

Tyler nodded. "I can go in the other room if you need privacy."

"No, stay."

Once she answered, Sergeant Oliver identified himself as the soldier she had talked to outside the headquarters of her father's former unit. "Ma'am, I wondered if you found any photos of your dad that we can use in the upcoming ceremony."

"Oh, Sergeant Oliver, I haven't had time. I'm so sorry. Give me another day or two if you don't mind."

"Certainly. Why don't I stop by tomorrow night? As I told you yesterday, we have a few military pictures, but I think some personal photos would be nice, as well."

"You're so kind to think of my father and to want to make the ceremony special. I promise I'll search through his papers and let you know if I find anything that might be appropriate."

"Appreciate your help, ma'am. It must be difficult going through his things."

"I'm not moving as quickly as I had hoped."

"No problem. Call me and I can pick the photos up anytime."

"Thank you, Sergeant Oliver." She hung up and informed Tyler of the sergeant's request. "I guess that means I have to go through his desk."

"If you want to look now, I could drop the pictures at his unit when I return to post this afternoon."

"But you wanted to talk to the Amish boy. Let's do that first. I'll check for photos later."

"Whatever you want."

She picked up the peach pie. "I want to take this to the Lapp family before Ruth bakes a pie of her own."

"I'll go with you," Tyler said. "I need to ask Isaac if he knows anything about Matthew Schrock."

The doorbell rang. Carrie looked quizzically at Tyler. "I don't have a clue who that could be."

Tyler led the way into the dining room and peered out the window. "It's Isaac and Joseph."

She called Bailey. "Joseph will want to say hello to you." When she opened the door, she realized the little boy wasn't here to play. His face was blotched from crying and his lower lip quivered.

"Isaac, is there a problem?" she asked, looking from the tearful Joseph to his stern-faced father.

"*Yah*, there is." He tapped his son's shoulder. "Tell her, Joseph."

"I am sorry for taking something that did not belong to me."

"Whatever are you talking about?"

Tyler came and stood behind her.

The little boy stretched out his hand and opened his fist. Lying on his palm was an old coin, covered with Georgia clay.

"I found this on your land. *Datt* said I should have given it to Mr. Harris."

"When did you find it?" she asked.

"Before Mr. Harris died. He is with the Lord now, so I kept the coin. *Datt* said I was wrong to keep anything that was not mine."

She held out her hand. The boy dropped the coin into her palm.

"You have been a very brave boy and done the right thing," Carrie said. "Thank you, Joseph, for returning what you found. Now I don't think you need to cry anymore."

"I am sorry."

"I know you are, and I have something that might help you dry your tears."

She stepped away from the door and grabbed the pie from the table. "Do you think your mother would like to serve peach pie tonight after you've eaten your dinner?"

He bobbed his head, the tears forgotten. *"Yah, ist gut."*

"Can you carry it home?"

His eyes widened. "I will be careful."

"You do not need to do this," Isaac said.

"It's a small token of my appreciation, Isaac. I'm grateful to have such fine neighbors. Thank you for helping my father and for helping me."

"That is what *Gott* would want us to do."

Tyler stepped onto the porch and pulled Isaac to the side.

"Joseph, take the pie to *Mamm*. Tell her I will be home soon," Isaac said.

When the boy was on his way, Isaac turned a worried gaze on Tyler. "Is something else wrong?"

"Matthew Schrock found the sergeant major's body. Do you know the boy?"

"Of course, I know him."

"Is the teenager truthful?"

Isaac nodded. "You can believe what he says. He is almost a man. What do you need to know?"

"Did you ever see the sergeant hunting on his property?"

"Often."

"What gun did he usually take with him?"

"Jeffrey had many guns. You have seen his gun cabinet?"

Tyler turned to Carrie.

"It's in his office," she shared.

"He told me he had recorded all his weapons," Isaac continued. "Many were old. Some antiques. He took pictures of them and wanted to be accurate in his details. There should be a binder with all the information about his guns."

"I'll look for the binder."

"I must go now and talk to Joseph. I do not want him to think that he is forgiven because he takes home a pie."

"But I have forgiven him, Isaac," Carrie assured the boy's father.

"The wrongdoing is forgiven, maybe, but he needs to make reparation for his actions. Sin carries a residual wrong that needs to be made right. He must help his mother and me until he has restored himself in our eyes. Then he will know he is forgiven. If forgiveness is given too easily, he will feel the sting later and the guilt will hang heavy on his shoulders. The next time he thinks of doing something wrong, he will remember if we do not make it too easy on him today."

"Don't be too hard on him, Isaac." Tyler took the coin from Carrie and rubbed away some of the red clay. "It's an old coin, but not that old. Joseph may have thought he'd found gold, but he didn't."

"If Joseph thought it was gold," Isaac said, "I fear he might have told his friends about the treasure he found. More rumors are not needed."

"He's a good boy," Tyler tried to assure him.

"*Yah*, but he will be a better boy when he learns to

obey his father." With a nod of farewell, Isaac turned and walked back to his house.

"Forgiveness is tricky," Tyler said, watching the man enter his home.

"I'm not sure I've forgiven my mother."

Tyler understood. "That's the way I feel about my father's death. Maybe we both need to make reparation."

"Meaning?"

"Maybe finding out how and why your father and Corporal Fellows died will bring peace. War was fought on this land. Many of your ancestors were wounded or killed in battle. Those traumatic deaths could pull the family apart for generations, until some type of healing takes place."

He looked at Carrie. "Maybe you're here to heal your family's past."

"And you, Tyler? Will you heal yours, as well?"

"I'm not sure."

TWELVE

"Let's check your father's office," Tyler said as he followed Carrie inside. They headed through the main living area to a rear hallway that led to a room with large windows, bookcases, a filing cabinet and, as Carrie had mentioned, a mammoth rolltop desk.

Tyler ran his hand over the rich hardwood, appreciating the workmanship and quality of the furniture. "It's old and has probably been in the family for generations."

"It could have been the desk Jefferson Harris mentioned in his letter, where he planned to hide a map to the treasure."

Tyler walked toward the side wall where a tall gun cabinet stood. "Your father had quite a collection of firearms. Just as Isaac said, some of them are antiques."

"I don't know guns, but I'll take your word for it."

"We need to find that binder."

Carrie turned around in a circle and threw up her hands. "Where should we start?"

"The desk." He glanced at her, knowing she was hesitant to delve into her father's personal items.

She stepped forward and slowly rolled back the top. The surface was clear of papers. She pulled open one of the small drawers and gasped.

Tyler moved closer. "What is it?"

"A picture of a woman holding an infant child." She stared down at the photo.

Tyler peered over her shoulder.

Her face clouded. She dropped the photo on the desk and turned away.

He rubbed his hand over her shoulder. "Have you seen that picture before?"

She nodded, her voice husky when she spoke. "My mother had a copy on the dresser in her bedroom. It was taken when I was three months old. She must have sent him a copy of the picture."

Tyler's heart broke for her. Her mother had manipulated a story that was untrue. "He kept it close, Carrie. That should bring you comfort."

She sniffed and shook her head as she turned to face him. "It brings more questions to bear. If he loved God so much, why didn't he try to find me, to have a relationship with me? All the years, he could have been in my life, but he remained distant and didn't try to see me. That's what I don't understand. It hurts not to be wanted."

"He kept the picture. He didn't exclude you from his heart."

"His actions don't prove that to be true, Tyler."

"He left you this house."

"Maybe he felt guilty as he aged. Or maybe as Isaac mentioned, it was reparation for abandoning me. Money or possessions weren't what I wanted growing up. I wanted a father."

Seeing the confusion and the pain on her face and the tears that filled her eyes, Tyler couldn't stop himself and pulled her into his arms.

She was soft and pliable and molded to him. The tears

fell. He felt her tremble and rubbed his hand over her shoulders as she cried.

Her grief tugged at Tyler's heart. He remembered the loss he had felt as a child at his own father's death. Carrie was grieving for a father she had always yearned to know.

For the first time, Tyler saw himself as the fortunate one. He knew he was loved. Somehow over the years he had forgotten the importance of that love.

At the moment, a stirring welled up within him of another type of feeling, a desire to protect and care for this woman who had been thrust into such despair. More than anything he wanted to right the wrongs and fix the hurts. If only he could.

He rested his head against hers and let her cry for the past, for the loneliness she had felt growing up, for her struggle with a mother who had been untruthful and for a future that probably confused her at this point.

Tyler knew deep within himself that he wanted her to turn to him in her need.

Was he asking too much?

Carrie wanted to remain wrapped in Tyler's arms. The pain she felt about finding the picture and knowing her father hadn't tried to contact her eased as Tyler pulled her even closer. Surrounded by the strength of him, she felt her grief start to ease. Perhaps she would be able to sort through her current confusion and find her way, with Tyler's help.

Selling the house didn't matter as much as finding who she was in relation to her father. Had he loved her from afar? As Tyler mentioned, at least her father had kept the picture of her close.

"Shhh," Tyler soothed. His voice caressed her heart and healed some of the brokenness she had felt for too long.

If only—

Realizing she was enjoying his nearness far too much, she drew back, unwilling to let her heart be swayed by a military guy. She didn't want to follow in her mother's footsteps. Carrie had to be careful, especially with a family history of betrayal.

Was that what had happened? Had her father betrayed her mother's love?

Knowing her mother's manipulative ways, she wondered if her mother had been the one to blame.

"I...I'm sorry," she stammered as she stepped out of Tyler's embrace. She felt an instant sense of loss, and the swirl of confusion returned to cloud her mind again.

She glanced at the photo. "I didn't expect to react so strongly. It's probably a combination of everything that's happened."

"You're allowed to be emotional, Carrie, seeing the picture of you as a baby and knowing your father had treasured it all these years."

She shook her head. "He probably stuck it in the desk long ago and forgot he even had the picture."

Tyler took the photo from her hand and turned it over. "What do you see on the back of the picture?"

"Smudges, darker patches."

"Caused by—"

"I'm not sure."

"Caused by the oil on his fingers. He had touched the photo countless time, Carrie, probably pulling it close to stare at his precious child."

She shook her head. "Yet he never contacted me."

Tyler let out a breath. "Maybe he didn't know where

to find you. Did your mother move? Perhaps she had given him the wrong address. The world was a different place back then, before computers and social media. Telephones and letters were the only ways to connect long distance. If your mother moved or changed her phone number, your dad could have lost track of both of you."

She sniffed and wiped her hand over her cheeks, feeling heat from her tears. "You might be right."

"I know I am." He carefully returned the photo to the desk drawer. "Why don't you make a cup of tea and sit for a while? I'll look for the catalogue of your father's weapons."

"But I need to help you, Tyler. There might be other things of interest that we'll be able to find together."

"Only if you feel up to it."

As much as she appreciated his thoughtfulness, she had to look through her father's things. The search would be easier having Tyler working at her side.

"Where shall we start?" she asked.

"The larger side drawers on the desk."

Together they opened the drawers and sorted through the files and papers, looking for anything that might mention the sergeant major's weapons or provide other clues as to her father's past.

Carrie found a number of sales receipts for work he had contracted on the house, for the kitchen renovations and the half bath downstairs. "I wonder if he did the remodeling because he planned to sell the house."

"Then changed his mind," Tyler added.

"Maybe we'll find something that gives us a clue of where he would have gone if the house had sold. From what most of the people I've met have said, my father seemed to be happy in Freemont."

"George Gates could have thought your father was more interested in selling than he really was. Now he's encouraging you to sell."

"Probably because his wife wants to change this into a bed-and-breakfast." Carrie looked through the windows to the hill at the rear of the property, the chicken coop and barn and what was left of the kitchen house. "I don't want strangers walking through this house or on this property, until I'm ready to say goodbye."

"You don't have to sell."

She nodded. "I know. But the estate tax will be significant. I'm not sure I can pay it."

"That's often the plight of farm families too and those who inherit a mom-and-pop business. The high taxes force families to sell land or a business just to have the money to pay the government. That's something you should convince Senator Kingsley to work on changing."

"You're right."

"Did you father have any other assets?"

"A few things that Gates said need to go through probate court. At least my father had the foresight to put my name on the deeds for the house and land so they go to me outright without having to be held up in court."

"Gates is providing information piecemeal, Carrie. You need to sit down with him and go over everything."

"He never has time and always says we'll cover the rest of the inheritance in a day or two."

"We can drive back to his office this afternoon."

"I'd rather talk to the Amish boy. I need to know how my father died."

Tyler glanced at his watch. "Let's search the office for half an hour. If we come up empty-handed, we'll visit Matthew and return later to continue looking."

"Didn't you say something about a meeting on post?"

"Later this afternoon. Do you want to come with me? You could wait in my office."

She smiled, appreciating his attempt to keep her safe. "I'll be fine. Bailey will be my watchdog. It's warmed up this afternoon. Maybe we'll go outside and see if Joseph wants to toss the ball. The thought of sitting in the rocker on the front porch would be a nice change of pace."

"As long as Isaac and Ruth are next door. If I'm tied up after dusk, be sure to come inside and lock the doors. Call me if you're worried."

"I'll be fine."

"Mind if I check the closet?" Tyler opened the door and glanced at the top shelf. "I may have found what we're looking for." He pulled down a large three-ring binder and placed it on the desk.

"Let's hope it provides the gun records," Tyler said as he opened the front cover.

The pages had plastic protective covers. "'A Collection of Weapons from the Harris Family,'" he read. "Exactly what we needed to find."

Flipping through the pages, he stopped a number of times to read the information about the various guns. "Your dad had lots of antique firearms. A few of them were passed down in the family. He purchased others at gun shows in the local area."

"Does anything stand out?"

Tyler came upon a photograph that made him pause. "Here's a picture of a Winchester Model 1894. Your father noted that it was his favorite gun to carry when he walked in the woods. The .30-30 caliber ammunition the police found in his vest would fit the rifle."

Turning the page, he found a photo of the sergeant major's gun cabinet. He lifted the binder off the desk, carried it to the wall and compared the photo to the actual guns on display.

"The Winchester is in the photo but missing in the gun rack."

"Is that proof enough that he had a gun with him the day of his fall?" she asked.

"No, but it provides a clue."

"If so, then what happened to the weapon?"

"That's what we need to find out. The rifle was old. Probably manufactured some time between 1894 and 1918, by the Winchester Repeating Arms Company in New Haven, Connecticut. In good shape, it could sell for over six thousand dollars."

Carrie's eyes widened. "Reason enough for someone to take the gun."

"Exactly. If the weather's good tomorrow, I'll hike up the hill and see what I can find."

"I'll join you. Bailey can tag along too. I'm sure he'd like to romp in the woods."

"And chase squirrels." Tyler smiled.

Carrie glanced at her watch. "Why don't we postpone looking for the photos of my father until later so we can visit the Amish boy?"

Tyler nodded. "Let's go now. Hopefully we'll find him at home."

Returning to the foyer, Carrie lifted her coat off the hall tree and turned to Bailey. "We won't be gone long." She nuzzled his neck.

As Tyler helped her with her coat, his hands lingered ever so lightly on her shoulders, causing an unexpected warmth to curl along her spine.

She stepped away from him, somewhat flustered. Her cheeks heated, and she glanced quickly at the hallway mirror to make sure she wasn't blushing.

"Is something wrong?" he asked, evidently oblivious to her unease.

"Just thinking of what we might learn today." True though her statement was, she was even more agitated by Tyler's touch. The memory of being wrapped in his arms was still so fresh.

When she had cried, he had comforted her, as any caring individual would do. She shouldn't read anything else into his embrace. It had merely been a compassionate response to her unexpected reaction after finding the photograph. Hadn't Tyler said as much?

Fumbling with the buttons on her coat, she stalled for time until her cheeks cooled and she could readjust her mindset.

Steeling her resolve, she reached for her purse. "Ready whenever you are."

He followed her onto the porch. She locked the door and walked with him to the car. Again he touched her arm as she slipped into the seat. Biting the inside of her cheek, she focused on the discomfort in her mouth instead of the ripple of response from his touch.

In DC, she had distanced herself from most men, other than those with whom she worked. They were older and married, except for the senator's senior adviser, who was recently divorced. Senator Kingsley was, as well.

In his early fifties, the senator had seemed more like the father she never knew rather than a boss. Although perhaps she had read too much into their relationship, especially since he still hadn't called to check on her.

Finding her cell in her purse, she glanced at the phone log to ensure that she hadn't missed his call.

"Has the garage phoned concerning your car?" Tyler asked as he started the engine and navigated out of the drive and onto Amish Road.

"I was checking. Not yet." Disappointment fluttered over her. Perhaps the senator hadn't received her message. She'd try to call him again later today.

"Did Isaac give you more specific directions to the boy's house?" she asked.

"He just said it wasn't far."

Finding the turn, Tyler pulled onto an intersecting dirt road that wound through a thick patch of forest. A clearing on the right revealed a small one-story house with a porch and side chimney. Chickens pecked at the grass, and a goat stood tethered near the house. The animal glanced up as Tyler turned onto the property and braked to a stop.

"The place needs paint," Carrie said, eyeing the slope of the front porch, the torn screen door and the window patched with cardboard. "And maybe a renovation crew."

Tyler nodded in agreement. "Looks like the Schrock family is struggling to hold on."

"There, Tyler." She pointed to a teenager who peered from the nearby barn. "That might be Matthew."

The boy approached as they stepped from the car. He wiped his hands on a rag and then tossed it over a nearby fence post. He wore the traditional Amish garb of a solid color shirt and black slacks, held up with suspenders.

A warning tingled Carrie's neck. She had seen the boy before, in town when she pulled out of the lawyer's parking lot the same day the lug nuts had been removed from her tire.

She glanced at Tyler and tried to silently warn him that something was very wrong about the house and surrounding land and especially the teenage boy with a pronounced limp who came to meet them.

THIRTEEN

One look at Carrie's face and Tyler knew something was wrong. He held her gaze for a long moment, then turned back to the Amish teenager limping toward them.

"Afternoon," Tyler said in greeting. He gave his name and introduced Carrie. "Are you Matthew Schrock?"

The boy glanced warily from one to the other. "What is it you want?"

"The police said you found Sergeant Major Jeffrey Harris's body in the woods. We want to ask you a few questions about that day."

"I told everything to the police."

"Ms. York is the sergeant major's daughter. She would like information about how her father died."

The boy kicked his foot into the dirt. His eyes held little compassion as he turned to her. "I do not know how your father died, but I'm sure his death was *Gott's* will."

Carrie didn't seem to buy in to his statement, but she nodded her thanks and then added, "You found him at the bottom of a hill?"

"That is right. I was in the woods and smelled death." He turned to Tyler. "You have smelled a dead animal? I thought it was a deer. I held my nose and stepped closer.

At first, I did not understand what I saw. So I walked around the body. On the other side, I could see the face."

"Was it bloodied?"

"Scratched and scraped from the fall. *Yah*, there was blood."

"Did you see anything that might indicate a fight had taken place?"

Again, the teenager glanced down and kicked a rock with his shoe.

"Matthew, did you hear me?" Tyler pressed. "Were there signs of a struggle?"

"The body fell down the hill."

"Yes, but could you tell if the deceased—the dead man—had been in a fight?"

"How could I tell that?" His glance was furtive as he looked from Carrie to Tyler.

"What was he wearing?"

The boy shook his head. "I do not remember."

"A hunting vest. Do you remember if it had a camouflage pattern?"

"Perhaps it was a vest."

"Did you see a rifle or any type of weapon lying nearby?" Tyler asked.

Again he shook his head. This time too hard and too quickly. "I did not see a rifle."

"How long did you stay with the body?"

"I did not stay. I ran to get help."

"You called the police?"

The teen nodded. "The Amish Craft Shoppe has a telephone. I called from there."

"Did you return with the police?"

"I had to show them where I found the body."

"Why were you walking in that area?" Tyler asked.

Again the furtive look. "I like the woods."

"But it wasn't your property, Matthew."

The boy's eyes widened. "I did not see signs about trespassing."

"You've taken that route before?"

The boy nodded. "Sometimes."

"Is there a friend you visit nearby?"

"Not friends. Just the woods. I like to be alone."

"Have you seen anything else in the woods when you walk?" Tyler asked. "Has anyone bothered you?"

Matthew frowned. "I do not understand."

"Have you seen soldiers or men fighting?"

The boy shrugged. "Maybe not."

"What does that mean, Matthew? Have you seen soldiers?"

"Sometimes."

"Have they talked to you?"

"Not to me, but to other Amish boys."

"What do the soldiers talk about?"

"About making money by doing jobs for them. Sanding, roofing, cutting lumber. They work on homes."

"Flipping houses?" Tyler asked.

"I'm not sure what they do."

"But they never asked you to help them?"

Matthew dropped his gaze. "Perhaps they do not think I can work hard."

"You know Eli Plank?"

"Yah."

"He said one of his friends saw two men fighting in the woods. Was that you, Matthew?"

"I saw something once. Through the trees. Two men appeared to be fighting. I turned away. It was getting dark. I needed to be home."

Tyler leaned closer. "Were the men in military uniform?"

"I could not tell."

"Was one of the men Jeffrey Harris, the man whose body you found?"

The boy glanced at Carrie. "I did not see their faces."

"When was the fight?" Tyler asked.

Matthew shrugged. "A day or two before I found the body."

"Was that why you returned to the area? Did you know someone had died?"

Matthew shook his head. "That is not why I was in the woods."

"Did you see a rifle when the men were fighting? Did you go back to find the gun?"

"I told you before. I did not see a rifle."

"Are you telling the truth, Matthew?"

A sharp dip of his head. "Why would I not tell the truth?"

"I don't know, but you won't get in trouble by telling us," Tyler said, hoping to reassure the boy. "I'll keep any information confidential. Do you understand?"

Matthew remained silent.

Tyler stared at the boy for a long moment before asking another question. "Did the soldiers invite you or any of the other boys to the cabin?"

Matthew's face paled. "What cabin?"

"Where soldiers watch movies and play pool. Have any of your friends gone there?"

"I do not see many people. There is much work to do at home."

"What about on Sundays, after services?" Carrie asked.

"My *Datt* does not always want to go. We must work."

"Matthew." The boy turned at the sound of his name.

An Amish man stood on the top of a small rise and stared down at the three of them.

"It is my *Datt*. He needs me."

"I live across the road from Eli Plank," Tyler said. "If you think of anything else, he'll know how to find me."

"I have nothing else to tell you."

"And I live in the old house next to Isaac and Ruth Lapp," Carrie added.

"And Joseph?"

"That's right. If you think of anything else, please let me know."

"Matthew," the father called again, his voice sharp and insistent.

"I must go." The boy turned and limped up the hill to where his father stood.

The man's hands were on his hips. He ignored his son and stared down at them.

"Might be time to leave," Tyler said, touching her arm. "Mr. Schrock doesn't seem friendly."

"Maybe he didn't like us talking to his son."

Getting in the car, Tyler turned to glance again at the hill. The boy had disappeared, but his father continued to watch them from the rise.

"I need to learn more about Mr. Schrock and his son," Tyler said once they were back on Amish Road.

"The boy may be keeping secrets," Carrie said.

Tyler nodded in agreement. "The father may have secrets, as well."

"Are we on for exploring the wooded area and hill tomorrow?" Carrie asked as they rode back to her house.

"What time?"

"Whenever you're free. Call me in the morning and

we can decide." She looked at the dark clouds overhead. "If the weather works in our favor."

Tyler turned into her driveway and braked. He hurried around the car, opened the door for her and walked her to the porch.

"Did you want to come in?" she asked as she unlocked the door.

He glanced at his watch. "I need to get to post. My boss likes everyone in their seats and waiting for him ahead of time."

"You'll be back before dark?"

"I never know. Sometimes he gets long-winded. Shall I call you when I get home?"

"Sure, unless it's really late."

"I'll call if your light is on."

When he hesitated, she stepped closer. "Thank you, Tyler."

He touched her hand. "See you tonight."

Her heart fluttered when he smiled. Did she notice a dimple? For the first time. What was wrong with her? Had she been so distracted that she hadn't noticed? She needed to make sure she didn't miss anything as noteworthy in the days ahead.

She stepped inside and waved from the window as he drove out of the drive and onto Amish Road.

Bailey stood with her, whining.

She leaned over and rubbed his back. "You need a little attention, don't you, boy?"

The dog barked, making her laugh.

"Is it dinnertime?"

He barked again.

"I know, you're hungry. So am I. Let's get dinner started."

Bailey trotted beside her and filled the stillness with

his warmth. She patted his head again and then filled his bowl with dog food. Bailey ate while Carrie pulled chicken breasts from the refrigerator.

"I'll cook extra in case Tyler is hungry when he comes home." The dog was much too interested in his food to respond to her comment.

Quickly she fixed a casserole, shoved it in the oven to bake and set the timer. She patted her leg for Bailey, who had finished his food and was sniffing around the oven, no doubt hoping for some chicken treats too.

"Let's look for those pictures Sergeant Oliver requested," she said to Bailey as she headed into her father's office. In the file cabinet, she found a manila folder marked "Photographs." She pulled it out and opened it on the desk. The photos were of her father, some in uniform on post and others in civilian attire in town. One was taken at the old train station and appeared to have been a ribbon cutting ceremony when he had donated the items to the new Freemont Museum. The docent they'd met stood next to her father.

Digging deeper, she found older pictures of her father as a younger man, tall and strong and handsome. No wonder her mother had fallen in love with him. Toward the bottom, she found a photo that tugged at her heart. Her father was standing with his arm around her mother, staring into her eyes. Both of them looked so very much in love.

Selecting a few of the more recent photos, she placed them in an envelope and wrote Sergeant Oliver's name and "Photos" on the front. She gathered the older pictures, including the one with her mother, and tucked them in her pocket so she could look at them later.

After returning the file, she and Bailey headed to the

front door. "Get your ball, and we'll sit on the porch and play."

The evening was peaceful with the smell of fresh earth and the first hint of spring. Bradford Pear trees were sprouting buds, and circles of daffodils were unrolling their leaves. Georgia was farther south than Washington, and Mother Nature, in spite of the cool temperatures, would soon burst forth.

Sitting on the porch, she tossed the ball into the yard and watched Bailey race to grab the toy and then bring it back to her and lay it at her feet like a trophy. She had to smile, and her outlook lightened at the dog's playful antics.

For an instant, she glanced at the other rocker and imagined her father—the man in the pictures—sitting next to her. If only she could hear his voice and see his facial expressions, more than what had been captured in the photos. She pulled the pictures from her pocket and looked at them again, trying to memorize the angle of his square jaw, the arch of his brow, the curve of his full lips.

A crow cawed, causing her to turn her gaze left to Tyler's neatly trimmed yard and pruned shrubs. A few daffodils had already opened, and the burst of yellow warmed her heart like sunshine peeking through the clouds.

Tyler was a good man and hardworking. He seemed to care about her and the plight she faced about whether to stay or sell the property. She sighed, thinking of sitting with him on the porch, seeing the firm set of his jaw as he surveyed the land she knew he loved as much as her father must have. She could see him turn to her and smile, showing the dimple in his cheek and the tenderness in his eyes that she noticed when he'd held her in his arms.

Again, a warmth swept over her, and she felt a serene peace and rightness envelope her, like his strong arms. His heart had beat loudly enough for her to hear the rhythmic pulse. Funny that she should think such thoughts of him when she'd started out questioning whether he could have been involved in the corporal's murder.

Within just a few days, she'd come to a new realization about many things, her father and Tyler and her mother. Carrie knew the importance of forgiveness. If she failed to forgive her mother, anger would fester and grow.

Bailey brought the ball and dropped it at her feet. Instead of playing, he returned to the yard and started chewing on something he found in the grass. Probably a stick or piece of bark.

"Bailey." He failed to acknowledge her call.

"Don't eat that," she chastised, brushing what looked like the last tiny remains of a piece of meat out of his mouth. "No, Bailey. Sit on the porch." He sat, nuzzled his ball and eyed a flock of birds that were swooping over a distant field.

Carrie breathed in the cool air and watched the twilight descend upon the farmland.

"Time to go inside," she finally said as the night turned chilly.

The dog eyed the Lapps' house as if waiting for Joseph.

"He's probably helping his mother with the dishes," Carrie said, thinking of Isaac's words about reparation.

Strict as Isaac seemed, his love for his son was evident. Ruth doted on the boy like most mothers. Would there be other children? Most Amish families were large. Surely Ruth and Isaac wanted more children, not that Carrie would broach the subject. She had been an only child and had longed not only for the father she had never known but also for brothers and sisters.

If she ever married and had a family of her own, she hoped for a number of children. Although reclusive women who closed men out of their lives couldn't expect to find someone special.

Again, she glanced at Tyler's house, then quickly turned her gaze back to Bailey. Rising from the rocker, she patted her leg. "Come on, boy."

The dampness of the night followed them inside where long shadows darkened the house. Carrie reached for a light switch and turned on the lamp. Even in the soft glow, she felt uneasy and returned to the door to check the lock.

The rich aroma of baked chicken and rice in a mushroom sauce drew her into the kitchen. Opening the oven, she peered at the bubbling casserole.

"It's almost ready." She smiled at Bailey, who sniffed the air.

Once the table was set, she pulled the casserole from the oven and covered it with foil to keep it warm.

"Everything's ready, Bailey. Let's wait in the living room?"

He stood at her side and wiggled with appreciation when she rubbed his back. "Tyler's meeting must be taking longer than he expected."

Glancing again around the kitchen and satisfied the dinner could wait, she turned off the light and headed for the comfy couch in the main room. Her father's leatherbound Bible sat on a side table. She pulled it onto her lap and opened the book. A paper fell out. She reached to retrieve it from the floor and startled at the handwriting she recognized. The return address confirmed what she had realized. The letter was from her mother.

Scooting closer to the light, she pulled the yellowed paper from the envelope addressed to her father, all too aware of her mother's script.

Dear Jeffrey,
You inquired about Carolyn and requested visiting me so you could see her. As I told you when you called, I do not want you to contact me again, and I do not want or need your help. Even more important, Carolyn doesn't need you in her life. You have been gone too long. I know you were overseas, but your inability to see her after her birth confirmed what I had always thought, that you weren't interested in our child. I insist that you stay away from us. We are moving. You won't be able to find us, so don't try. If you do try to contact us, I'll call the police and tell them that you have been causing problems. I know you had hoped my feelings would have changed, but they haven't. I thought you would get out of the military. When you accepted your overseas assignment, I saw you for who you really were, and that wasn't someone I wanted associating with my child.

Carrie's heart broke. Her father had wanted to see her, but her mother had stood in his way. After returning the letter to the envelope, she tucked it back in the Bible along with the photo of her mother and father.

Her eyes burned. Through the veil of tears, she retraced her steps to the kitchen and put the casserole in the refrigerator before she climbed the stairs to the bedroom. Bailey trotted at her side.

How could her mother have been so thoughtless to

separate her from her father's love? The pain swept over her and clamped down on her heart. She pushed open the bedroom door and fell onto the bed. Bailey dropped to the floor beside her.

Hot tears fell from her eyes. She pulled tissues from the box on the nightstand and held them to her eyes. She cried until her head throbbed and she had no more tears, only shallow sobs that caught in her throat.

Her swollen eyes hurt. Her heart hurt even more. She didn't want to stay in Freemont, yet she didn't want to leave. All she wanted to do was forget today had ever happened and cry herself to sleep.

FOURTEEN

The howling wind woke Carrie from a fitful sleep. She groped her hand across the nightstand, searching for the electric alarm clock that usually lit the night.

Touching the lightless clock, she fidgeted with the dials, but to no avail. Raising her hand, she searched for the lamp switch and turned the knob. The room remained dark.

A quiver of concern wrapped around her throat. She sat up and listened. Bailey lay at the side of the bed, his breathing deep and labored.

"Bailey?" She touched the dog, who failed to respond. "Bailey, wake up."

Her worry turned to fear when he didn't move.

Again she groped her hand across the nightstand. Relief washed over her when her fingers touched her cell phone.

The screen lit. She found the flashlight app and shone the light on Bailey, yet he failed to rally. She touched his nose. Cool and moist. Was that a true indication of a dog's health and well-being?

Searching her phone log, she hit Tyler's number. Surely he was home by now. The call went to voice mail.

"It's Carrie. Something's wrong. I can't wake Bailey. And the electricity is off. I was asleep. There must have been a storm. Call me."

Stepping around the dog, she padded across the bedroom and opened the door to the upstairs hallway. Peering over the railing, she glanced at the first floor entryway, but saw nothing except the faint outline of furniture below.

The house was in the country where power outages were probably a norm. Perhaps a faulty generator or a malfunction of some sort. She'd find the number to the electric company in the kitchen phone book and notify them of the problem.

Again she turned on the flashlight. The light dimmed. As she checked the battery, her heart sank. Her battery needed to be charged. Without electricity, she wouldn't be able to use her phone.

She glanced at her phone again. Why hadn't Tyler returned her call?

Grabbing the banister, she started down the stairs. A sound made her pause halfway to the first floor.

Nerve endings on high alert, she turned her head toward the rear of the house. What had she heard?

The settling sounds of an old house?

Or something else?

The sound came again. Like a drawer opening.

Her neck tingled and her stomach roiled.

Another creak. A footfall?

Someone was in the house.

Heart pounding, she hurried down the stairs and turned toward the kitchen, determined to leave through the back door and run to Tyler's house.

If he was home.

Footfalls sounded in the hallway, coming closer.

Her chest tightened. Fear strangled her throat and escalated her beating heart.

No time to flee. She needed to hide. But where? In spite of the darkness, she felt exposed.

Another creaking floorboard. Close. Too close.

She ducked behind the sofa and hunched down. Her body trembled, and her heart pounded too loudly.

A series of footfalls moved into the main room. She held her breath. He grunted, as if more animal than human. Fear clung to her. She wanted to whimper, but any noise would draw his attention.

Another step, then another.

He was so close she could smell him.

Stale beer and sweat.

Afraid to breathe, she crouched even lower.

He walked in front of the couch, two feet from where she was hiding. If he went into the kitchen, she'd make a dash for the front door. Could she make it in time? The lower lock would need to be turned and the dead bolt released.

Grip the knob, twist and pull the door open. Run.

The Lapps' house would be the closest. Were they home? Awake? Would they hear her pounding on the front door, and if so, would they come to her aid?

What about Tyler?

Tied up with a meeting on post.

Now or never. She started to rise. Her cell phone trilled. Glancing down, she saw Tyler's name on caller ID.

The intruder turned, lunged. His hand caught her shoulder.

She screamed and fumbled with her phone, trying to answer the call.

"Carrie?" Tyler's voice.

The intruder knocked the cell from her hand.

"No!" she screamed.

He grabbed her hair and jerked her head back. She thrashed her hands to strike him.

He raised his hand and slapped her across the face. She reeled and crashed against the wall. Air whooshed from her lungs.

Groaning, she crumbled onto the floor and crawled away from him, sobbing with fear.

He kicked her in the ribs.

She moaned, rolled into a ball. He kicked again.

Knowing she had to fight back, she grabbed his shoe and twisted his foot. He fell against the couch.

Scrambling to her feet, she ran. He followed, his footfalls heavy on the hardwoods.

Unsure of herself, Carrie took the corner to the kitchen too fast. Her feet slipped, slowing her down.

His hand clamped down on her arm. He threw her against the doorjamb. The hinge dug into her back.

"Oh!" she gasped, then ran forward. On the counter was a knife that she had used earlier to slice the chicken.

Grabbing the handle, she turned and raised the blade.

He caught her hand in a death grip and tightened his hold, bringing tears to her eyes and making her legs weaken. She sank to one knee, fighting to keep hold of the knife that was raised precariously over her head.

She…didn't…have…the…strength…

He twisted her arm.

She screamed in pain.

The knife dropped. She shoved it across the floor before he could stoop to retrieve it, then struck him in the face.

He growled and went for her neck. She backed against

the counter. His grip tightened. She couldn't breathe and gasped for air.

Tyler!

She had to open the door and scream for help.

Tyler would save her.

But hands tightened on her throat, and her lungs burned like fire.

She couldn't scream, she couldn't move, she couldn't see and as she slipped into another place, she realized she wouldn't live to breathe again.

Irritated that the CID meeting had taken so long, Tyler increased his speed after leaving Fort Rickman. Glancing at his phone resting on the console, he debated calling Carrie, then checked the clock on the dashboard. Ten o'clock. Too late.

Carrie was tired and probably in bed sound asleep. The last thing he wanted was to wake her. They'd talk tomorrow.

But he couldn't stop himself from reaching for his phone. Using his one hand, he punched in his security code and swiped to access his screen.

A new voice mail.

Concern swept over him. He'd turned his phone to vibrate during the meeting and placed it in front of him on the conference table, yet he had missed the incoming call.

Tyler touched the prompt and raised the phone to his ear.

"Something's wrong with Bailey… The lights are out."

His pulse raced. He pressed down on the accelerator and pushed Call.

She answered, but what he heard sent chills through his heart.

Carrie's scream, along with the sounds of a scuffle or worse.

He tossed the cell aside, gripped the steering wheel and raced through town. He had to get to Carrie.

Never had the drive seemed so long or the road so winding.

He breathed with relief when he reached Amish Road, but his heart stopped when he saw the Harris home in the distance, standing dark against the night. He screeched into the driveway and jumped from the car, his weapon raised and at the ready.

Pounding on the front door, he screamed her name. Circling the house, he saw the French doors open and a man, running into the woods. Much as he wanted to pursue the intruder, he had to find Carrie.

"Carrie!" He tried the light switch that didn't work and raced into the main part of the house.

The sound of the dog's footfalls came from overhead. "Bailey, come. Where's Carrie?"

The dog failed to appear, which added to his concern. Tyler ran from room to room, fearing the intruder had harmed Carrie and her faithful pet.

Entering the kitchen, he stopped short seeing her on the floor. He knelt beside her and touched her neck. Relief swept over him when he felt a pulse.

Hurriedly he called 911. "Emergency. Medical help needed now."

After providing the necessary information, he disconnected and rubbed his hand lightly over Carrie's cheek, seeing the welt and marks from the assailant's hand. A cut on her lip was oozing blood, along with a scrape to her forehead and another to her hand.

She moaned. A good sign.

"Carrie, it's Tyler. I'm here. The intruder's gone. You're safe with me. Open your eyes. Talk to me."

She moved her hand.

"I know you're in pain. The ambulance will arrive soon. You'll get medical care, but you need to let me know you can hear me. Open your eyes, Carrie. I need to see your eyes."

Her eyelids fluttered.

"That's right, hon. Open your eyes."

He gripped her hand, relieved when she squeezed his fingers. "I know you can hear me."

"Ty—"

"Good job. I'm right here. Open your eyes."

Again, her eyelids fluttered, then opened for a second before closing again. He lit a candle and placed it on the counter.

"Try again," he encouraged.

Her eyes opened ever so slightly. He smiled. "I see you."

Her lips twitched as if she wanted to smile.

He patted her hand. "I'm going to check your pupils."

Gently he pulled back the eyelid on her right eye and then the left one. The pupil and iris looked normal. No severe dilation. Hopefully that meant no concussion.

At least that was in her favor.

Sirens sounded in the distance.

Footsteps on the front porch. Someone pounded on the door.

Carrie's face twisted with fear.

"I'll check it out. It's not the assailant. I saw him running into the woods. I'll be right back."

More pounding.

Tyler raced into the foyer, peered through the window and was relieved to see Isaac.

"Carrie has been hurt," he said as he opened the door. "An ambulance is on the way."

"I saw your car. The door was open, and the lights were on. I knew something had happened."

"Someone broke in and attacked Carrie."

Isaac's face clouded. "They hurt her?"

"I'm afraid so. She was unconscious when I arrived, but she opened her eyes and tried to let me know she could hear me."

The two men hurried to the kitchen.

Tyler bent down next to Carrie. "Isaac is here. The ambulance is close. Hang on."

She nodded, almost imperceptibly.

"Did you see your attacker?"

She shook her head. "Mask."

"He wore a mask over his face?"

She nodded.

Flashing lights invaded the kitchen.

The sound of car doors and men climbing the front steps. Isaac hurried into the foyer and pointed them to the kitchen.

Tyler stepped aside as the EMTs entered, hauling medical bags and a stretcher. He quickly filled them in on what he knew.

"An intruder. Looks like Ms. York was beaten. He ran from the house as I pulled into the driveway."

Knowing Carrie was in good hands, he stepped into the foyer and met Officer Phillips there.

"Did you see the perpetrator?" the cop asked.

"Only as he was running into the woods," Tyler said with regret. "I could have chased him, but I was worried about Carrie and rightfully so. He wore a mask and messed her up pretty badly."

"What happened to the power?"

"He must have cut the line." Tyler thought suddenly of Bailey. "And tranquilized the dog."

Borrowing a flashlight from one of the officers, Tyler headed upstairs and found Bailey lying in the hallway. He appeared sleepy but otherwise all right, which was a relief. If the perpetrator had given the dog a sedative, it had been short-lived.

Tyler checked the bedrooms and saw the aged journal on the nightstand near the bed where Carrie had been sleeping. Had she heard a noise and gone downstairs to check it out?

Returning to the hallway, he patted his leg. "Come on, Bailey. Let's have the medics look you over after they finish with Carrie."

The dog slowly rose and padded after Tyler, who kept his hand on his collar in case Bailey's legs buckled under him. Thankfully the dog went down the stairs without any problems. He trotted into the kitchen, whined at the cluster of people around Carrie and wiggled his way to her side.

Her hand rubbed against his fur. "Are you okay?" she managed to ask.

He wagged his tail.

"Looks like the dog may have been given something that knocked him out," Tyler told one of the medics who took Bailey aside and examined him.

"He seems okay, sir. His eyes are clear. His reflexes are good."

"What about Ms. York?"

"We're taking her to the hospital in Freemont. The doc may order a CT scan. Her vitals are good, but she's got a knot on her head, a bruised cheek and what may be a couple broken ribs."

"I'll follow in my car."

He found Isaac. "I'm going to the hospital with Carrie. Would you stay here with the police?"

"Of course. Tell Carrie we are praying for her recovery."

"Thanks, Isaac. She needs prayers."

Phillips motioned for Tyler to follow him to the rear of the house. "Check out the sunporch. Looks like your intruder was looking for something."

Tyler hadn't noticed the chaos earlier when his thoughts were on finding Carrie. Now he saw the scattered papers and books and other memorabilia tossed about the room.

"Wonder if he found what he came searching for," Tyler mused.

"No telling." Phillips picked up an old plat of the property that had fallen out of a manila envelope. "Did you see this?"

After stepping closer, Tyler studied the plat. "It's of the Harris property."

Opening the drawer on the desk, he was relieved to find the photograph of Carrie still in place.

"Something important?" the officer asked.

"One of Carrie's baby pictures."

"What about the journal the firemen found the other night?"

"It's upstairs in one of the bedrooms," Tyler said. "I wonder if that's what the guy was looking for. She probably came downstairs never expecting someone was in the house."

The cop flashed his light over the porch door. "Looks like he got in through the French doors."

"And Bailey wouldn't have heard because he was drugged, which meant the guy had to have been in the area earlier. Carrie had planned to sit outside and let Bailey play. He may have found something edible laced with sleeping medication."

Returning to the living area, Tyler approached Isaac. "Did you see anyone hanging around the house today?"

"The boy who fed the chickens. Matthew Schrock came with him."

"Anyone else?"

"Not that I saw."

Phillips signaled to Tyler. "The EMTs are ready to transport her."

"I'll follow the ambulance. Isaac Lapp will stay in the house until your folks are ready to leave."

Tyler hurried to his car in time to pull behind the ambulance as it raced back to town.

In the rearview mirror, he could see the flashing lights of the police sedans for miles. The strobe effect added a chilling reality to the dark night.

Someone was after Carrie. He—or she—had almost killed Carrie tonight. Tyler hadn't been there, which frustrated him.

As a boy he'd wanted to help his father, but he'd been unable to save him. The reason he went into law enforcement had been to help people in need. Carrie was in need, and Tyler had been worried about her security, yet he hadn't been able to protect her.

What did that say about his ability?

As the Amish said, he was *dummkopf*. Stupid. Not worthy of wearing the uniform and not able to keep Carrie safe.

FIFTEEN

Carrie didn't like hospitals, especially when she was the patient. The emergency room doctor was thorough in his evaluation and had ordered a CT scan to ensure that her injuries weren't life threatening.

Much as Carrie's body ached, she was all right. A few scrapes and bruises, a sore rib and a pounding headache that made her grit her teeth and clench her fists, but she would survive.

Thanks to Tyler.

She peered out the door of the examination room when the doctor left and smiled when she saw Tyler standing in the hallway.

He stepped closer. "Do you want company?"

"That sounds good, although I'm not much for conversation at this point. My head's throbbing, and I keep telling myself that I should have been smarter. How's Bailey?"

"Doing fine, the last I saw him. Isaac stayed at the house to watch over everything. The doc will let you go home as soon as the blood test results are back."

"What happened to the electricity?"

"The guy cut the line coming into the house."

"He wanted me in the dark."

"Your dad's office papers were scattered about. He may have been looking for the diary."

She nodded. "It was upstairs in the guest bedroom."

"When I pulled into your driveway, he must have exited through your dad's office."

"Good riddance."

"Exactly, but we need to find out who it was and why he was there."

"Land or treasure would be my two guesses," Carrie said through half-closed eyes.

"He may have been after you."

Carrie kept thinking of Tyler's comment as he drove her home. Had the intruder entered the house to do her harm? If she hadn't gone downstairs, would he have climbed to the second floor and attacked her there?

She shivered thinking of what could have been on his mind. Biting her lip, she blinked back tears as the memory of his vicious blows swept over her again.

Tyler touched her arm and worked his hand to hers. His fingers tightened as if he read her mind and wanted to comfort her. "You've been through a lot, Carrie."

"All my life, I longed to know about my father. I never expected information about him to come with such a high price."

"Your father didn't want this to happen."

"But was he involved, Tyler? I keep thinking it can't be coincidental."

"Have you found anything in the journal?"

"Only that things were hidden somewhere on the property. Charlotte called them her treasures, but she never mentioned gold."

"Yet her husband's letter at the museum mentions coins that needed to be secreted away."

"Could all of this—the two murders and the attacks, my tires, the chickens—" She glanced at Tyler, hoping he could make sense of what she was trying to say. "Could they all have been caused by one man's greed?"

"I'm not sure at this point. Your father's death could have been accidental, yet Eli said his friend had seen men fighting. The sergeant major usually carried his rifle when he walked in the woods. It wasn't recovered when his body was found. Did someone kill him and take the rifle?"

"Maybe Fellows."

Tyler nodded. "That could be, but if so, then who killed Fellows and why?"

"What if the corporal was searching for buried treasure? Someone else could have been working with him," Carrie mused.

"The guy who eventually killed him."

She nodded. "If everyone's after the same thing, and they thought my father knew how to find it, they could have been fighting among themselves."

They rode in silence as Carrie thought back over the events that had led to this point in time. Tyler seemed equally lost in thought.

He let out a deep breath when the outline of the old antebellum home appeared in the darkness. After parking at the side of the house, Tyler opened the driver's door.

Isaac walked toward the car, Ruth hurrying along behind him.

"She is all right?" the Amish man asked.

"Thankfully nothing was broken. She'll be sore for the next few days, but it could have been so much worse."

"Thanks be to *Gott*," Ruth said.

Carrie could hear them talk even though the windows were raised. Opening the door, she waited. Tyler hurried to help her from the car.

Ruth stepped closer and wrapped Carrie in her arms. "We were so worried." The Amish woman's embrace had a motherly quality that brought comfort and a sense of homecoming.

"You cannot stay alone in your father's house," Ruth said. "Isaac and I both insist that you sleep at our house. We have an extra room. You will be safe there."

Isaac nodded in agreement. "No one will think to look for you in our house."

Carrie glanced at Tyler. "I don't want to give in or let the attacker think he's won."

"Your safety is our first consideration," Tyler said. "I don't want you staying alone in your father's house after someone was able to get inside. Tomorrow I'll fix the back door, install more security and get the power turned on, but for now you need to stay with the Lapps."

"What about Bailey?" Carried asked, glancing at the house.

"I brought him earlier into our home," Isaac assured her. "I wanted to watch him through the night because of the drugs he had in his body. He didn't seem as playful as usual, and I was worried about him. He is in Joseph's room, curled up on the floor by his bed. The boy loves him, and the dog is happy there. I will check on both of them later."

Relieved that Bailey was in good hands, Carrie realized she needed to accept the Lapps' offer and stay with them.

She turned to Tyler. "You'll be all right?"

"Of course. I need to contact the local police and CID on post and try to put together any new information they've received. Plus, I'll keep an eye on your house, Carrie, while you rest."

She shivered as wind blew through the trees, and a sliver of moon broke through the clouds. Tyler was right, but she didn't want to leave him.

Stepping closer, she said, "Thank you, Tyler, for coming to my rescue today."

He wrapped his arms around her and drew her close for a moment. His embrace warmed her.

"I'll see you in the morning," he whispered, dropping a kiss on her forehead before he pulled away.

Ruth took her hand. "Come, Carrie. We'll go to my house now."

Carrie glanced over her shoulder as she walked with Ruth. Tyler waved and gave her an encouraging smile visible in the moonlight.

For one frightening moment, she wondered if she'd see him again. Then shaking off the thought, she followed Ruth into the house. The smell of fresh-baked bread and the oil from the lamps greeted her.

"You would like something to eat before you go to bed?" Ruth asked, her eyes filled with concern.

"I'm fine, but tired. Are you sure you have room for me?"

Ruth nodded. "Upstairs. I have a nightdress you can wear and soap and water if you would like to wash your face and hands."

She lifted a small lamp from the nearby table and motioned Carrie to follow her up the wooden stairs.

The door to the first room was open. Ruth paused

and pointed to the bed where Joseph slept. "Look where Bailey is."

Carrie peered inside. The dog rested on a small rug at the side of the boy's bed.

Ruth smiled. "Joseph will be surprised when he wakes in the morning."

Bailey opened his eyes. Spying Carrie, he walked to the door, tail wagging as he nuzzled her leg. She bent to pat him, finding comfort from his welcome.

"Good to see you, boy," she whispered so as not to wake Joseph. "I was worried about you."

"Your room is this way." Ruth pointed to the end of the hallway.

Bailey followed the two women into the small but pretty guest room. A single bed was covered with a quilt. Two fluffy pillows were encased with white pillowcases embroidered with tiny spring flowers. A newly laundered nightdress lay folded on the nearby washstand that also held a basin and pitcher of water. A package of wrapped toiletries added a thoughtful touch that Carrie appreciated.

Curtains covered the windows in a delicate subdued print that matched some of the quilted patches on the spread. Wall pegs provided a place where Carrie could hang her clothes.

"If you need anything, just call for me. I will be sleeping across the hall. Isaac will be watchful throughout the night. You do not need to worry. Our doors are locked, and Isaac will not let anyone intrude. You are safe here."

"Thank you, Ruth. You and your husband have done so much for me."

"We are grateful for your friendship. Your father helped us when we first moved here. He sold some of his land so Isaac could have a nice farm. That meant so much to us."

She placed the lamp on the stand.

"Sleep well," Ruth said as she left the room and closed the door behind her.

Bailey whined.

"You want to go back with Joseph?" Opening the door, Carrie watched the dog walk to the end of the hallway. He glanced back as if to ensure that she was all right before he entered the boy's room.

Overcome with exhaustion, Carrie went to the window and pulled back the curtain. She could see her father's house and a corner of Tyler's one-story ranch beyond. A light came on in one of the rooms, and even from this distance, she could see someone standing at the window and staring out into the night.

She doubted Tyler could see her, and she wondered what he was thinking. She didn't know her own mind at this point, but her heart reached out to Tyler. Grateful as she was for the Lapps, she was even more grateful for him. Tyler had tried to protect her and keep her safe. But someone was still out there.

Her gaze moved to the dark stand of trees at the rear of her father's house and the spot where she'd stumbled upon Corporal Fellows's body. After all that had happened, the police were no closer to finding his killer. Nor did they fully understand the reason for her father's death or who was attacking her.

Should she stay longer and risk her own life? Or should she return to Washington? In DC, she wouldn't have to worry about a killer in the night, but that meant leaving Tyler.

Would he care if she left?

Carrie thought again of the comment he'd made when she mentioned not wanting to leave the Lapps. "What about the neighbor on the other side?" Tyler had asked.

Perhaps he wanted her to stay after all.

Tyler looked out the window and stared at the Amish house. While most of the dwelling was blocked from view, he could see one of the upstairs rear windows where a faint light glowed. In his mind's eye, he envisioned Carrie at the window staring back at him. Foolish to imagine such a thing. Tired as she was, Ruth had probably already tucked her into a bed piled high with handmade quilts and fresh, dried-on-the-line linens.

As much as Tyler wanted to believe otherwise, Carrie wasn't thinking of him. If she was thinking of anything, it would be her job in DC and the speech she needed to write for Senator Kingsley.

Had the senator changed over the years? Surely since his drinking had been such a significant problem back then, he would have sought treatment and stopped the addictive behavior by now.

The memory of his father's death returned with the screech of tires, the crash of metal and the horrific sound of his father's scream as he called Tyler's name. Along with the wail of sirens and the flashing lights came the memory of a closed-casket funeral and of a young boy who wanted to see his father again.

Tyler turned from the window as his cell rang.

Seeing Everett's name, he connected and raised the phone to his ear. "Anything new on the case?" he asked in greeting.

"I got a call from the first sergeant at the engineer battalion. One of the guys in the unit started talking. Evidently a few of the men had visited a cabin not far from Amish Road. They'd check out of post on a three-day pass to work for a guy in town who flips houses. He's got a cabin where the soldiers stay so they don't have to drive back and forth to Fort Rickman. The construction boss stocks the fridge with beer and wine, and provides X-rated movies to entertain the men at night. From the way the soldier talked, it sounds like it's in the vicinity of the Harris home."

"Was Fellows involved?"

"He helped sometimes. Guess the money was good. They were paid in cash so everything went into their wallets with nothing taken out for Uncle Sam."

"Is the soldier willing to share names?"

"Not yet, but we plan to haul him in for questioning."

"I'll head to post sometime tomorrow." Tyler filled Everett in on what had happened at Carrie's house. "She's staying with one of the Amish families tonight. I need to find out more about that cabin. I'll call the local police and see what they can uncover."

After disconnecting, Tyler called Phillips. "You're working late," he said when the cop answered.

"Sounds as if you are too. How's Ms. York?"

"I'm guessing that she's fast asleep at the Amish neighbors' house. Staying in her father's place again was too risky."

Tyler explained about the soldiers and the cabin where they crashed and then asked, "Do you have any knowledge of a cabin and who might own the property?"

"I'll search the county records and get back to you," Phillips said. "We don't show anything on our maps of the area. The guy must keep information about the cabin off the radar. As you know, there are a number of dirt roads that twist through that area. They have to lead somewhere."

"Check out Nelson Quinn."

"The real estate agent?" Phillips asked.

Tyler nodded. "Quinn sometimes flips houses. Also check on Mrs. Gates and the mayor's wife."

"Will do. By the way, I contacted a friend who will reconnect the power first thing tomorrow."

"Thanks. That saves me time and means I can hike Harris's property in the morning."

"Let me know what you find, and, Tyler—"

"Yeah?"

"Watch your back," Phillips warned. "The attacks are escalating against Ms. York. I have a hunch the killer's becoming desperate, and we both know that when a killer's cornered, he often strikes again. I don't want you in his crosshairs."

"I'll be careful. My main concern is Carrie. She didn't plan on being a target and keeps wondering if it involves her father."

"That's been my question as well," the cop said. "But everything I've learned about Jeffrey Harris is positive. The guy kept to himself, was unassuming and was the first to lend a hand when someone was in need."

"Let's hope you've got it right."

Tyler disconnected and began searching the archives of the local paper for any history of the area that might have a bearing on the investigation. Sometime after midnight, he found a picture of the Harris home as it was when the sergeant major's elderly aunt had lived there, until her death.

By then, the house had fallen into disrepair. The restoration must have been extensive and costly. How had Har-

ris, on a sergeant major's paycheck, afforded the work?
Maybe Carrie's hunch would prove true. Maybe her father was involved in something corrupt. Could he have taken part in the weekend construction projects that involved the soldiers in his former unit?

As much as Tyler didn't want anything negative to surface, he needed to learn the truth.

Reading through a feature story about the renovation, he found mention of a builder, named Ulmer, who had helped with the project.

Where had he seen that name?

Tyler poured a cup of coffee and stared again at the house next door. Once he'd downed the strong brew, he grabbed his jacket and walked around the Harris home, checking that the doors were locked and the property secure.

The sounds of the night surrounded him. In the distance, an owl hooted, its deep call adding to the sense of unrest he felt. He glanced at the wooded area behind the house and the hill beyond. Was there a cabin out there someplace, and if so, was the killer holed up inside, waiting and perhaps watching?

Lord, help me solve this case. The words slipped through Tyler's mind and surprised him. He had closed the Lord out of his heart since his father's death, but being with Carrie had renewed his faith, at least a little.

He stared at the Lapp house. His gaze homed in on the upstairs rear bedroom where he'd sensed Carrie's presence.

He had changed since her arrival. For the better.

Maybe after all these years, it was time to leave the past behind and make his way into the future unencumbered by the anger and distrust that had hovered over his heart for too long.

"Forgive me, Lord, for not being able to forgive another." Perhaps forgiveness would come in time. Right now he was grateful for being open to the Lord.

If he remained around Carrie, he might find his heart soften even more. She had an effect on him. A good effect. She forced him to look beyond his own broken past and see the potential of a future free of resentment, a future based on love.

He shook his head. Carrie brought feelings of protectiveness and an almost constant desire to be near her. Was that love?

Only time would tell. Would she stay in Freemont long enough for Tyler to make sense of his emotions or would she return to DC and to the senator who wasn't worthy of her attention?

SIXTEEN

Carrie woke with an aching body. The bumps and bruises she had received from the intruder seemed even more painful this morning. Groaning, she dropped her feet to the floor and stood, feeling the blood leave her head. The room swirled around her. She grabbed the headboard and waited until the dizziness passed. As if sensing her presence, Bailey pushed open the door and stepped into the room.

"How are you?" Carrie patted his nose and scratched his back. "Did you sleep well in Joseph's room?"

Hearing his name, the boy knocked lightly on the door and peered into the room. "Is Bailey with you?"

"Come in, Joseph." The boy was all smiles as he entered and knelt on the floor. Wrapping his arms around the dog's neck, he whispered, loud enough for Carrie to hear, "I couldn't find you, Bailey."

The boy's words touched Carrie's heart. That was how she felt about her father. She couldn't find him, couldn't find who he really was. Then she thought of everything people had told her. Why couldn't she accept what they had said? Instead she continued to question whether her father was involved in something corrupt and illegal.

How foolish of her. As if blinders were removed from her eyes, she saw more clearly. Her father was a good man. He had wanted a relationship with his only child, but he had honored her mother's wishes. Perhaps he felt at fault for not being the father he should have been, for not marrying her mother and for forcing her to raise a child outside of marriage. For a man who embraced the Lord and scripture, that could have been a heavy burden to carry that would have brought a sense of unworthiness.

She felt unworthy as well and was overwhelmed with a desire to connect with her heavenly Father. *Lord, forgive me for accusing You of not loving me, when I was the one who rejected You. Open my heart to love You more.*

Thoughts of her mother came to mind, a lonely woman who was never satisfied with her life or her daughter. Carrie didn't feel anger or resentment, but a sadness that her mother had never experienced the peace Carrie felt at this moment.

Joseph leaned back against the bed and brushed against her leg. Bailey snuggled close, enjoying the boy's hugs.

Carrie's heart opened even more completely to the goodness she felt in this house, to the warm embrace of love from the Lord and her new appreciation for both her earthly father as well as the God of heaven and earth.

Love filled her for her father, for the Lord and—

The face that came to mind made her startle.

Tyler?

He had worked so hard to protect her and keep her safe. He made her smile, and she felt protected and totally at home in his embrace.

Was it… Could it be love?

"Joseph," Ruth called to her son.

The boy jumped to his feet. "You're staying for breakfast?" His eyes were wide and hopeful.

"I would like to, Joseph."

"Can Bailey stay too?"

"If your parents agree."

"I'll ask *Mamm*." The boy scurried out the door.

Bailey looked up at her with his big brown eyes as if needing her consent. She laughed and hugged him. "Go with Joseph. I'll be fine."

The dog hurried from the room.

Carrie slipped into the clothes she had worn yesterday and folded the nightgown Ruth had provided. After making the bed and smoothing the quilt covering, she moved to the window and pulled back the curtain. In the distance, she saw Tyler heading into the thick woods behind her father's house. No doubt, he was in search of the cabin the Amish boys had mentioned, knowing she wouldn't feel up to hiking across her father's property this morning.

Keep him safe, Lord. Let him find the cabin and information about my father's death so the case could be solved and the investigation ended.

A sadness swept over her as she thought of what that would mean. Tyler would move on to the next case, and she would return to Washington and the life she knew. She'd sell the house and forget about Freemont and the Amish community and the family legacy she had found in South Georgia.

Would she… Could she forget about Tyler?

Grateful for the old plat Phillips had found in Carrie's father's office, Tyler followed the markings on the brittle yellow paper. He discovered a path, probably where deer ran, and followed it to the steep rise from which Carrie's father had fallen. Glancing over the drop-off, he was all too aware that a fall could have broken the sergeant major's neck. A soldier, trained in hand-to-hand combat, would have known how to inflict the same injury, as well.

He glanced again at the plat and noted the end of the sergeant major's property, but continued walking for half a mile farther. Peering through the woods, he saw a structure in the distance and had a surge of exuberance, knowing he might have found the cabin the Amish boys had talked about and the soldiers had mentioned.

A path, wide enough for a single vehicle, led toward the main road. He and the Freemont police had searched, but the woods were vast and dense and the trail had eluded them.

Nearing the cabin, he glanced through the windows. A number of cots filled the main room, along with a large-screen television and pool table. Chances were the refrigerator was stocked with beer.

Spying something else, he pulled out his cell and called Phillips. "I've found a cabin that needs to be checked. Through the window, I can see a rifle. Looks like a Winchester 1894, the model the sergeant major carried when he was in the woods. Ammo was found in his pocket, which means Harris was probably carrying the rifle. The person who took the Winchester could have been the man who fought the sergeant major. If we find the owner of the cabin, he might lead us to the killer."

By noon, Phillips and his men had gotten a search warrant and had scoured the cabin for evidence. The rifle appeared to have belonged to the sergeant major, although ballistics testing would confirm ownership. The gun, like the rest of the cabin, had been wiped clean of prints. When the police wrapped up their investigation, Phillips gave Tyler a drive back to his house.

"Thanks for your help," he said as Tyler stepped from the car.

"Carrie will be glad we found the cabin and the gun. I'll tell her now."

He hurried to her house and tapped on the door. She answered looking tired. Bruises darkened her cheek and forehead.

"How are you feeling?" he asked, stepping inside.

"Better than last night."

"Were you able to get a good night's sleep?"

She nodded. "Which was what I needed. Ruth insisted I stay for breakfast, and I ate more than I have in years. Her ham and eggs and fresh-baked biscuits and gravy were wonderful. If I lived with them long, I'd weigh a ton."

She tried to laugh but grimaced. Raising her hand, she brushed her fingers along her jaw. A dark mark outlined one of the strikes against her face and brought Tyler back to the subject at hand.

"I found the cabin," he said. "The police retrieved what we think is your father's missing rifle."

"Who owns the cabin?"

"We don't know yet. Phillips is trying to find the records for the property. He's concerned that the deed for the land may go back further than the recorded county documents. They may need to access some of the old records in the county courthouse."

"So we don't know who the attacker is yet?"

"Soon, Carrie. It will all be over soon."

"Do you want some coffee?" she asked.

"Sounds good. Evidently your power's back on."

"For which I'm thankful."

On the way to the kitchen, he saw her laptop on the dining room table and a few papers scattered close by. "You've been working?"

She nodded. "On the speech for Senator Kingsley."

He let out an exasperated breath.

"I know you don't like him," she said.

"He's not a good man, Carrie."

After grabbing two mugs from the cabinet, she poured coffee and handed a mug to Tyler. "The senator is not against the military."

"I'm not referring to his present political stand. I'm referring to something that happened years ago."

She looked confused. "What are you talking about?"

"I told you about the car crash that killed my father."

Carrie nodded.

"I never told you who was driving the other car."

Her gaze narrowed. Her voice weak when she spoke. "Drake Kingsley?"

Tyler nodded. "He was drunk, Carrie, and staggered from his car. My father was dying, I was cut and bleeding and Kingsley called someone who picked him up. The next I knew he was exonerated from any wrongdoing. He killed my father and walked away without being prosecuted."

"That's why you went into law enforcement," she said.

He nodded. "And why I don't want you involved with the senator."

"But that was years ago, Tyler. He's a changed man."

"Is he?"

"I've never seen him drunk."

"Maybe he's reformed. I hope so, but I still question his judgment and integrity. Tell me you'll quit your job."

She took a step back, seemingly perplexed by his comment. "I...I can't do that."

"If you stay here, you could find another job. Maybe on post."

"It's not the same."

"You mean it's not Washington. That's it, isn't it? You're not interested in small-town Georgia."

"You said it yourself, Tyler. I've worked hard to get where I am. I can't throw it all away."

He smiled ruefully. "I wouldn't want you to throw your career away, Carrie. I just want you to think of what you've found in Freemont that you won't have in Washington."

She looked around the house. "I've found an antebellum home that I don't want to live in alone, Tyler. Yes, I know more about my past, but that's not enough moving forward. I need something else in my life."

"You need Washington."

His cell rang. It was Phillips. "We've got a name," the cop said. "Karl Ulmer. His wife, Yvonne, comes from an old Freemont family. The cabin belongs to them. We're going to haul them both in for questioning."

Tyler disconnected. "They found the connection." He told Carrie the names and that the woman was old Freemont.

"Yvonne is the docent at the museum," Carrie said.

Tyler nodded. "I knew I recognized the name. Her husband did some refurbishing for your father after he acquired the property when his elderly aunt died. Ulmer must have seen the potential then. When your father retired, folks thought he'd leave Freemont. Ulmer wanted to buy the house and land. He's probably the person who

Flo mentioned that wanted to turn this area into a rec-reational site."

"Which the Amish would never want."

"Are you still planning to sell?" Tyler asked.

"Not to them, but I'll find a buyer, someone who will care for the house."

"Really, Carrie? Who's to say the next buyer won't sell to someone else for the right price? Your legacy will be gone, cut up into a housing development or even shops and restaurants like these people planned to do. Think about Isaac and Ruth Lapp. That's not what they want for this area."

"I can't take care of everyone, Tyler. I have to take care of myself."

Tyler bristled at the sharpness of her tone. "That isn't what I wanted to hear."

He turned his back on her and strode to the door. "I need to go back to post and inform the CID what's happening. The Ulmers had a motive and appear to be involved in your father's death. You should be safe, since the couple is in custody. Still, keep your doors locked." He glanced around. "Where's Bailey?"

"He stayed with Joseph. I plan to give the dog to him when I leave."

Tyler's gut tightened hearing her say the words that cut into his heart. This had all been of so little value to her, when it had meant so much to him.

He glanced at the table by the door and saw the envelope for Sergeant Oliver. "You found photos of your dad?"

She nodded. "Last night."

"I'll stop by the unit and get these pictures to Oliver." Opening the door, he turned to stare back at her.

"Looks like everything's over, Carrie. You can make arrangements to leave. I'll watch over your property until it sells."

He stepped outside and heard the door slam behind him. Hurrying across the yard to his car, he struggled with a mix of regret and heartache, which he hadn't expected. Carrie had finally made up her mind. She was leaving Freemont and leaving him.

Slipping behind the wheel, he pulled onto Amish Road and never looked back at the Harris home or the woman who would leave him and return to DC, taking his heart with her.

SEVENTEEN

Tyler found First Sergeant Baker at the unit and handed him the photos. "These go to Sergeant Oliver. They're pictures of Sergeant Major Harris."

The first sergeant scratched his head. "That's strange."

"Why?" Tyler asked.

"Oliver and the sergeant major were at odds," the first sergeant explained.

"Since when?"

"Since the sergeant major discovered Oliver arranging payday loans with some of the guys in the battalion."

"Where'd Oliver get the money?"

The first sergeant stepped closer. "From what I heard, his brother-in-law was the source of the loan money. Oliver was the middleman. Of course the interest rate was sky-high."

"Using soldiers who worked under him for his own personal gain is against regulations," Tyler said, stating the obvious.

"Yes, sir. That's why the sergeant major brought the situation to the commander, who gave Oliver an Article 15, which meant he didn't pass his promotion board. Without a promotion, Oliver couldn't reenlist. He's leaving the military at the end of the month."

"But he's working on the ceremony honoring Harris at the end of the month?"

The first sergeant shook his head. "That's something I haven't heard. Oliver is an ornery guy who can pick a fight at the drop of a hat. I can't see him working on a project that would honor the sergeant major."

A sick feeling settled in Tyler's midsection. "Where's Oliver?"

"He signed out on a three-day pass. He mentioned visiting a friend in Florida."

"Do you know his brother-in-law's name?"

The sergeant thought for a moment. "I should. Seems he earned his money in real estate."

"Quinn?" Tyler offered. "He's got a real estate business in Freemont."

"Maybe." The first sergeant pursed his lips. "But I can't be sure. I'll think of it in a minute. Are you going to be around?"

"I'm heading to CID headquarters." Tyler gave the first sergeant his cell number. "Call me if you remember the name."

Carrie's heart had broken when Tyler walked out the door. The story about his father's death troubled her deeply. Could it be true?

She stared at her computer monitor for long enough to know that she couldn't move forward until she talked to Senator Kingsley. Finally she reached for her cell and called Washington, hoping to learn the truth.

The senator's senior adviser answered.

"I want to talk to Senator Kingsley," Carrie demanded.

"No can do, Carrie. What's the problem?"

"Why isn't he returning my phone calls?"

"The senator's tied up."

"Something's going on, Art, and I don't like it."

"What about the speech?" he asked.

She glanced at her laptop and the blank screen on her monitor. "I'll have it done in time."

"I want it ahead of time, Carrie."

"I've never missed a deadline," she said, feeling frustrated and somewhat helpless. "I need to talk to the senator. Now."

"I told you—"

"Look, Art, there's something important from his past that I need to discuss with him."

"What's it involve?"

"A two-car accident some years ago."

The adviser sighed. "Who told you?"

She didn't understand his change of direction. "Who told me what?"

"You're talking about the accident that killed a single dad who had a ten-year-old son, right?"

"Is it common knowledge?" Carrie asked.

"It may be soon enough. Some news reporter called the senator for a statement. He plans to feature the story in *The Washington Post* this weekend. That's why the senator finally decided to take matters into his own hands."

"I don't understand."

"Do I have to spell it out for you, Carrie?"

"I guess you do."

"Rehab." Art's tone was sharp. "The senator checked into a treatment center for alcohol addiction."

His words felt like a stab to her heart. "I…I never thought he had a problem."

"You never socialized with him, Carrie. He was on his

best behavior at political functions. Socially and away from the office was a different story."

"What about the speech I'm supposed to write?" She glanced again at her laptop.

"He'll be out of rehab by then. So write it, Carrie, and send it to me as soon as it's finished so I can be sure it reflects the senator's wishes."

"All this time, Art, have you been the one pushing the antimilitary sentiments?"

"I've counseled the senator."

Anger welled up within her. "You've controlled him."

"The senator needed someone."

"He didn't need your hateful feelings about the military. Why can't the senator voice his own mind?"

"Because he's weak, Carrie. I'm the power behind Drake Kingsley."

"Shame on you."

"You may not realize, Ms. York, that the world is filled with lots of people who can write speeches. Jobs are hard to come by in this downward economy. I wouldn't be quite so quick to express an opinion contrary to your boss."

She steeled her spine. "My boss is Senator Kingsley."

"I'll tell him how you feel."

"Fine, but I'll write the speech and email it prior to the deadline. Tell him I'm praying for his return to good health."

She hung up tasting the bitter bile that rose in her throat. Art was hateful. She'd had blinders on her eyes all this time, like some of the horses that pulled the Amish buggies. How could she have been fooled by the senator? Thinking back, she realized Art was right. She had never socialized with the senator or any of his staff. The few functions she attended had been job related when, evidently, he was on his best behavior.

Thankfully the senator was getting the help he needed. *Oh, Lord, help him.* She sighed.

The doorbell rang.

Expecting to see Joseph and Bailey, she hurried to open the door.

"Sergeant Oliver." She took a step back, surprised. "I didn't expect you this early."

"I told you I'd stop by for the pictures."

"Tyler Zimmerman took them to the unit. I'm sorry you had to make a trip for nothing."

He stepped inside, although she hadn't invited him in. A sense of déjà vu filled her.

"It's not a problem," he said. "Besides, I wanted to talk to you about something else."

"Oh?"

"The treasure."

She tried to smile through stiff lips. "Which probably doesn't exist."

"You know where it's located," the sergeant insisted.

"Rumors in town have gotten out of hand," she assured him. "That was long ago, and I doubt there would be anything of value to find, even if there had been treasure."

"Corporal Fellows told me he had found a coin."

A tingle curved along her spine. "You mean the soldier who was killed?"

Oliver nodded and stepped closer. "He'd found the stash, but he wouldn't tell me where it was located."

She took a step back and glanced at the table where her cell phone lay. The memory of the attack last night swept over her.

"Tyler might know about the treasure." She reached for the phone. "I'll call him."

Oliver slapped the cell out of her hand. "Don't try that again."

Her eyes widened. "You were here last night."

"Looking for the maps that I couldn't find. The letter at the museum in town said Jefferson Harris would leave a map for his son, only there weren't any in the desk. Where are they?"

She turned and fled into the kitchen, hoping to reach the side door. Surely someone would hear her if she got outside.

He grabbed her hair.

She screamed and fought back.

His hand rose, just as last night, and she tensed, anticipating the blow that rocked her world.

The pain made her gasp for air. She doubled over. He kicked her in the stomach. Air *whooshed* from her lungs.

She collapsed onto the hardwood floor, thinking of the women of old who had washed the floors by hand.

She'd never finished reading the journal or learned what happened to her ancestors. Before she could think anything more about the past, darkness swept over her, wiping out the pain and the memories.

Before he got to CID headquarters, Tyler's phone rang. "Zimmerman."

"Sir, this is First Sergeant Baker with the engineer battalion. I remember the name of Oliver's brother-in-law. It's Ulmer."

Tyler's gut tightened. "You're sure?"

"Yes, sir."

Tyler thanked the first sergeant and tried Carrie's

phone, but it went to voice mail. As he headed off post, he called Everett and quickly filled him in. "Put out a BOLO for Sergeant Frank Oliver. Supposedly he's heading to Florida on a three-day pass, but that could just be a cover. I'm driving back to Amish Road to warn Carrie."

Next he contacted Phillips. "See what Ulmer has to say about his brother-in-law. I need to warn Carrie. She's at the house alone."

"I'll send one of our men to check on her," Phillips assured him.

Tyler arrived at the house before the police. He pounded on the door and then circled to the rear and broke through the French doors, just as the intruder had done.

"Carrie," he screamed.

The house was empty, but he found her cell phone on the rug and spattered blood on the kitchen floor. Heart in his throat, he retraced his steps.

Joseph was in the backyard.

"Go inside, Joseph. Tell your dad that a soldier from post may have taken Carrie into the woods. Stay with your mother. Tell her to lock the doors."

Fear clouded the boy's face. Tyler hated to scare him, but the boy needed to be kept safe.

Tyler raced toward the woods. He had to get to Carrie. He had to get to her in time.

"Tell me where the treasure is buried," Oliver insisted. His voice was low and menacing.

He had brought her to a dark, dank cave on the side of the hill where her father must have fallen to his death. Fallen or been pushed.

She squared her shoulders, looking defiantly at the sergeant. "I don't know anything about treasure."

"I heard one of the new volunteer firefighters in town was reprimanded for talking about a journal that mentioned buried treasure."

She shook her head. "The clues provided in the little book have long since disappeared. One was a twisted oak, the other a hedge of blackberry bushes. Both are gone."

He raised his brow. "A twisted oak. There's one not far from here. Two trees have grown together. The trunks wrapped one around the other."

"Then maybe that's where you should look," she suggested, hoping to turn his thoughts to anything except her.

He grabbed her arm. "You're going with me."

"No." She shook her head. "I can't help you."

"Of course you can. You can dig, and then when the treasure is unearthed, you can crawl into the hole and I'll bury you."

Fingers of fear clutched at her throat. "No," she whimpered.

He grabbed a shovel and pushed her toward the mouth of the cave.

She screamed. The sound was chilling, but who would hear her?

Not Tyler. He was at Fort Rickman tying up the loose ends of the investigation.

Oliver slapped her face. She grimaced with pain but remained upright, determined to appear strong and in control.

"I know about the cabin," she said, hoping to focus the sergeant on anything except killing her. "It belongs to Karl Ulmer."

Oliver sneered. "Karl's my brother-in-law. He had big plans for developing your father's land."

"With a shopping mall."

"That's right. Until the sergeant major found out he was related to me. Then your father decided to keep his land. Karl blamed me when the deal went south. I had to prove that I could take care of myself, and I wanted my sister to be proud of me."

"By stealing what belongs to someone else? Fellows found a buried coin, and you thought it was part of the treasure. Is that why you killed him?"

"Fellows found a coin when he was planting shrubbery. He'd seen the light on in the big house and was headed there to tell you about his find."

"So you did kill him."

"I had to," Oliver insisted. "Fellows planned to tell you about my search for the treasure. He knew I'd argued with your father. He thought I'd killed the sergeant major even though I told him it was an accident."

"But you did kill him," Carrie insisted.

Oliver smirked. "I wanted him to die after what he did to me. I shoved him, knowing he wouldn't be able to stop his fall."

"You're a murderer."

With a shake of his head, the sergeant added boastfully, "I'm a man trying to provide for my future."

"By killing two innocent people."

He slapped her again. She fell to the ground.

"Drop the gun, Oliver."

The sergeant turned at the sound of his name.

Tyler stood in the clearing, his weapon raised.

The sergeant grabbed Carrie and shoved the gun to her head. "I'll kill her if you take one step closer."

Tyler's gaze narrowed. "You won't succeed."

"Try me," the sergeant taunted.

Carrie struggled to free herself.

"Bailey." Joseph's voice.

Ice chilled her veins. Out of the corner of her eye, Carrie spied the boy standing wide-eyed, openmouthed.

"Joseph, run home. Fast." Tyler's warning.

Bailey growled and raced forward. He nipped at Oliver's leg.

Carrie jabbed her elbow into the soldier's gut and shoved him hard.

He fired.

The bullet hit the ground just inches from her foot.

She kneed his leg, throwing him off balance. He pulled her down under him. She grabbed his wrist, unable to gain control of the weapon.

Tyler clamped his hand down on the sergeant's shoulder, lifted him off Carrie and kicked the weapon out of Oliver's hand.

"Augh!" the guy screamed, his hand limp.

Picking him up by the collar, Tyler jammed his fist in his gut.

Air rushed from the soldier's lungs. Oliver collapsed on the ground, holding his stomach and moaning in pain.

Raising his weapon, Tyler took aim. "You move, Oliver, and you die. Understand?"

The sergeant nodded.

Tyler reached out a hand of support for Carrie. "Are you all right?"

She steadied herself against his sturdy frame. She hurt all over, but she was alive and so was Tyler.

"Where's Joseph?" She searched the bushes, worried about the boy.

"I am here," he said, waving at both of them.

"Joseph?" Isaac's sharp call came from the path.

The Amish man stepped into the clearing and opened his arms for his son. "You were to stay home."

"Bailey got out. I had to follow him. He knew Carrie was in danger."

The police were right behind Isaac and quickly took Oliver into custody.

Tyler holstered his weapon and wrapped both arms around Carrie. "Are you sure you're not hurt?"

"I'm fine now," she said, resting her head on his shoulder.

The fear that had surrounded her eased. In Tyler's arms, she was safe.

Officer Phillips approached. "When my patrolman found the Harris home deserted and the French doors standing wide-open, he called for backup. Sorry it took so long to find you." He glanced at Joseph with his arms around Bailey. "If not for those two, we might have gone in the wrong direction."

"Oliver pushed my father to his death," Carrie told them. "He also killed Corporal Fellows."

"The sergeant had a reputation of being a hothead," Tyler shared. "Even without your father getting involved, I doubt he would have been promoted."

Officer Phillips nodded in agreement. "Your father had declined the offer Ulmer made, Ms. York, but not because of Oliver. Your dad wanted to hand the property on to you, his only child. When Oliver learned the deal wouldn't go through, he became irate. Ulmer feared that he'd sought out the sergeant major and pushed him down the steep incline to his death."

"Matthew had witnessed the fight and went back later to check on your father," Tyler mentioned. "Oliver hadn't seen him."

"Unfortunately Ulmer didn't go to the authorities with the information about his brother-in-law," Phillips added. "That won't bode well for him when he comes up on tax evasion charges. Plus, he took part in Oliver's payday loan schemes."

"What about his wife?" Carrie asked.

"The two of them were probably working together," Tyler said. "I'm not sure what the judge will decide, but I am sure of one thing. He'll throw the book at Oliver. The sergeant won't have to worry about what he'll do after retirement from the military, because he'll be doing time."

Phillips lifted his phone. "If you'll excuse me, I need to notify the chief."

He stepped away, leaving Tyler and Carrie to themselves.

"Seems we were interrupted a bit earlier." He smiled.

"Interrupted?" she asked.

"That's right. Officer Phillips interrupted us. You were in my arms, and I was planning to kiss you."

"I wouldn't want to spoil your plans," she whispered, moving closer and lifting her lips to his.

His kiss was warm and lingering and took her breath away. When he pulled back, her knees went weak, and she grabbed his arms to keep from falling.

"You're not okay."

"I'm fine, just light-headed, but it doesn't have anything to do with my injuries."

"Then what caused the problem?" His lips curved into a knowing smile that showed his dimple and warmed her even more.

"It must have been your kiss."

"I know of only one solution for that problem, ma'am."

"Oh?" she asked, feigning innocence. "What's that?"

"Another kiss." He lowered his mouth to hers and they melted together in a long and luxurious embrace that made the world stand still and everything else fade into the background.

Why had she thought of leaving Freemont? She'd found her home. She was at home in Tyler's arms.

EIGHTEEN

Tyler paced in front of the War Memorial. He was part of the contingent of military police and CID special agents waiting for the ceremony honoring Freemont veterans to begin.

He checked his watch and searched for Carrie. "Have you seen her?" he asked Everett.

"Be patient, my friend. She won't miss this occasion."

Tyler couldn't help being nervous. He'd been tied up on post yesterday and returned home too late to call Carrie last night. The large, stately home had been dark, and at the time, he thought she was already in bed asleep.

This morning, he'd driven to post early to coordinate the military police presence at the ceremony that would honor the local veterans. General Cameron and CID Chief Wilson wanted to ensure that nothing, no matter how seemingly insignificant, detracted from the solemnity of the day.

When Tyler had called Carrie earlier, her phone had gone to voice mail. Now he was frustrated that he hadn't knocked on her door last night to ensure that she was all right.

She still wasn't sure about whether to return to Washington, especially because of the senator's important speech. Carrie had spent the last few days fine-tuning the talk. Hopefully she hadn't been forced back to DC at the behest of her boss.

The army band stood at parade rest near the grandstand. The bandleader tapped his baton and called them to attention. On the count of three, they began to play a jaunty military march that had the people gathered in the seating area tapping their feet in time to the music.

Again he glanced at his watch.

Everett beckoned him forward to help with the video screen. "Let's adjust this a bit higher so everyone can see the slide program. Didn't you say they were planning to honor Carrie's dad?"

"That was the plan, but with Oliver in jail, no telling what the photos will highlight."

"The first sergeant said he's got it covered," Everett assured him.

"I hope so."

The *clip-clop* of horse hooves sounded. Tyler turned toward the main street. What he saw made him smile.

Joseph waved from the buggy and sat next to his father in the front. Bailey was tucked in at the boy's feet.

Behind them sat Ruth and next to her was Carrie.

Tyler hurried to help Isaac harness the horse to a post, and then he helped Carrie down. His hands lingered on her waist as he lifted her effortlessly to the ground. "I didn't know if you were still in town."

"I wouldn't miss this," she said with a smile. "Ruth and Isaac asked if I wanted to accompany them. After all they've done for me, I thought it would be fitting."

"There are seats reserved for you and enough for the Lapps, as well."

Tyler escorted them to the front of the VIP area.

Bailey sat between Carrie and Joseph. "You'll join us, Tyler?" she asked.

Everett overhead her question and smiled at Tyler. "You're on the guest list, my friend. Your place is next to Carrie. You don't want to disappoint the lady."

Carrie handed him a sealed envelope when he sat down.

"What's this?" he asked.

"A letter from Senator Kingsley. I got one too. Open it. You have time to read it before the ceremony begins."

Unsure of what the letter would contain, Tyler tore open the envelope. The handwritten letter expressed the senator's sorrow at the accident so long ago that had taken Tyler's father's life. The senator claimed full responsibility for the accident. He had gone to rehab and was trying to restore the brokenness he had caused. Knowing that nothing could replace Tyler's father, the senator had decided to step down from public office and donate a sizable contribution to the creation of a program to help kids at risk. He had been a kid without a father to guide him, and he had taken Tyler's father from him. He wanted to help other young men overcome the anger that could lead to a life of addiction, anger and dependency.

He planned to name the organization the Zimmerman Alternative in honor of Tyler's father. In the closing paragraph, the senator asked Tyler's forgiveness.

The anger Tyler had felt for so long disappeared.

He turned to Carrie. "I never expected this."

"Neither did I. This morning he gave the speech I wrote—a patriotic and pro-military speech. At the end, he included a special statement and texted me the video."

She pushed a few prompts on her phone. Senator Kingsley stood on a podium with an American flag at his back and concluded the speech Carrie had written for him. The applause was instant and heartfelt.

"I have something to add," the senator said to the audience. "I need to ask forgiveness for my actions years ago." He went on to talk about his condition that night, and the accident that had taken an innocent man's life. "What I did was wrong. That I didn't turn myself in was wrong, as well. That's why I'm turning myself in today and asking the state to try my case so that justice can be served. I am stepping down from my senatorial seat. I am not worthy to follow in the footsteps of honorable men who have served before me, and I ask your forgiveness. Whatever the verdict, I pray that no one will suffer like the Zimmerman family, and especially Special Agent Tyler Zimmerman, who lost his father years ago."

Carrie's smile was wide as she reached for Tyler's hand and held it tight throughout the ceremony honoring the local veterans and especially commemorating her father, Sergeant Major Harris.

When the slide show concluded, Carrie turned to Tyler. "I know my father was a good and honorable man who loved the Lord and worked to help others whether through the military or civilian life. He did his family proud, and I'm proud of him."

She squeezed Tyler's hand. "I'm proud of you, as well."

George Gates approached them. "Mind if I interrupt?"

"Not at all," Carrie said as she and Tyler stood.

"Did you check out the safe-deposit box?" the lawyer asked.

Carrie nodded. "And the savings account at the bank. My father had done well with his investments as you mentioned."

"All the paperwork has been filed, and the rest of the estate should go through probate soon. You won't have long to wait until everything belongs to you. I presume you're keeping the house and property."

"That's right." She glanced at Tyler and smiled. "I'm staying in Freemont for a long time."

Back at the house following the event, Carrie prepared a lovely lunch and invited the Lapps to join them. The neighbors recounted heartwarming stories about the sergeant major that brought more than a tear to Carrie's eyes. By midafternoon, the neighbors had said their goodbyes. Tyler helped Carrie with the dishes and then told her to change into walking shoes so they could go for a hike in the woods.

"But why?"

"Trust me."

Which she did.

Hand in hand, they crossed the field where Corporal Fellows's body had been found and entered the wooded area.

"We're going back to the twisted tree?" she said.

Tyler smiled. "That's where Oliver thought the treasure was buried. But I read the journal found in the kitchen house, and with the help of the old plat realized the twisted oak wasn't the end of the treasure hunt but the beginning."

"If we're going to dig for treasure, we should have brought a shovel," Carrie said, wondering what Tyler had planned.

"I don't think we'll need one."

Finding the twisted oak, Tyler pointed west. "What do you see?"

"The steep hill that we're going to climb?"

"Exactly." Tyler ushered her to a side path that led almost to the top.

"What do you see now?" he asked once they stopped to rest.

"The entrance to the cave."

"Which was hidden for years. I noticed it on the old plat. When Oliver tore through the vines and undergrowth, he did us a favor."

Carrie peered inside the dark opening.

"Follow me." Tyler motioned her forward.

"This doesn't bring back good memories."

He squeezed her hand. "You may change your mind."

Turning on the flashlight, Tyler angled the light into the far recesses of the cave where a small opening appeared. "Hope you're not frightened by small spaces."

"Would it make a difference?"

"You could stay here and wait for me."

She shook her head. "No, Tyler, we're in this together."

His smiled widened. "I like that."

He hesitated for a moment and lowered his lips to hers. "Excuse me, ma'am, but I thought a kiss was in order."

Not that she objected.

She would have rather stayed and continued kissing him instead of bending low and entering the smaller confined area.

The flashlight played over the interior chamber.

Tyler sighed with discouragement.

"What's wrong?" she asked.

"I thought—"

The light caught on a dirt-covered object. "There." He pointed and motioned her to follow him to where a small rectangular box sat.

Kneeling, Tyler brushed his hands over the surface. A cloud of dirt and dust filled the air.

"It's a trunk," she gasped, realizing what they'd found.

Tyler undid the latch and slowly lifted the lid. He shone the light into the interior.

Carrie pulled out a faded quilt and unwrapped a teapot that had been carefully nestled within the fabric. The weight of the pot and the tarnished facade made her realize it was probably sterling. Quickly she unwrapped a coffee urn and cream and sugar accompanying pieces.

"Charlotte Harris wrote about her tea service." Carrie glanced up at Tyler. "We've found her keepsakes."

He angled the light into the truck. "There's more." He handed her two objects.

"Silver candlesticks," Carrie said. "They're beautiful."

A small box lay nestled in table linens. Carrie gasped when she opened it, seeing the cameo brooch surrounded by seed pearls. "It's exquisite."

"No gold coins, but treasures nonetheless." He drew out a leather-bound Bible.

Carrie read the names listed inside. Charlotte Jones and Jefferson Harris and their children.

"It's a family tree," she said to Tyler.

He put his arm around her shoulder and drew her close. "It's your family, Carrie."

"But I want a real one, Tyler. Not just the memories."

He hesitated and then his face softened. "We haven't known each other long, but I want a family, a family with you, Carrie. You can say no if you want to go back to Washington, but I hope you want to stay here. I want you to be my wife."

"Oh, Tyler," she sighed.

"We can take our time, but I love you, and want to spend the rest of my life holding you in my arms."

"That's what I want too."

She glanced at the Bible. "We'll write our names in the family tree. Tyler Zimmerman and Carrie York Harris wedded into married life."

"There's space for the names of our children," Tyler added with a smile, before he kissed her.

Slowly they walked back to the Harris home. Carrie wore the cameo, and Tyler carried the trunk filled with the family treasures.

In the field behind the house, they spied Joseph running toward them with Bailey at his heels. "Guess what?"

"You're so excited, Joseph." Carrie laughed. "Do you have a surprise?"

"*Yah. Gott* is giving me a baby brother or sister."

Carrie's heart burst with joy at the good news. "Oh, Joseph, that's wonderful."

"I told *Mamm* I'd been praying for a baby harder than I was praying for a dog."

"It sounds as if God answered the best prayer of all," Tyler said, smiling at the boy.

"He answered both prayers." Joseph motioned them forward. "Look what's in the box on the front porch."

Tyler placed the trunk inside the house and then joined Carrie on the Lapps' porch.

Peering into the box, she smiled.

"It's a puppy," Joseph squealed. "An Irish setter like Bailey. *Mamm* said they will be best friends if you stay here."

"Don't worry, Joseph." She took Tyler's hand. "I'm staying here. I wouldn't leave this area for anything."

She looked at the house and the small boy and the dog and then into Tyler's eyes. "Everything I love is here."

Then as Joseph and Bailey played and the puppy frolicked nearby, Tyler and Carrie sat in the rockers on the porch of her father's house and enjoyed the evening breeze and the smell of the flowers blooming as spring arrived in Freemont—the first of many springs they would have together. They'd be together for a lifetime of seasons that would take them from today across the years when children of their own would play in the yard. They'd add their names and the names of their grand-children to the family Bible so the rich heritage of the Harris-Zimmerman family would continue on…forever.

* * * * *

Dear Reader,

I hope you enjoyed *Plain Danger*, the ninth book in my Military Investigations series, which features heroes and heroines in the army's Criminal Investigation Division. Each story stands alone, so you can read them in any order, either in print or as an ebook: *The Officer's Secret*, book 1; *The Captain's Mission*, book 2; *The Colonel's Daughter*, book 3; *The General's Secretary*, book 4; *The Soldier's Sister*, book 5; *The Agent's Secret Past*, book 6; *Stranded*, book 7; and *Person of Interest*, book 8. Carrie York inherits an antebellum home in Amish country from a father she never knew and ends up in the middle of a murder investigation. When the killer comes after her, she needs CID Special Agent Tyler Zimmerman to keep her safe, but both of them struggle with issues from the past. If you feel burdened by past pain, ask the Lord to open your heart to His mercy and love so, like Carrie and Tyler, you too can live happily ever after.

I want to hear from you. Email me at debby@debby giusti.com. Visit my website at www.DebbyGiusti.com, blog with me at www.seekerville.blogspot.com and at www.crossmyheartprayerteam.blogspot.com, and friend me at www.facebook.com/debby.giusti.9.

As always, I thank God for bringing us together through this story.

Wishing you abundant blessings,
Debby Giusti

REQUEST YOUR FREE BOOKS!

2 FREE RIVETING INSPIRATIONAL NOVELS
PLUS 2 FREE MYSTERY GIFTS

Love Inspired®
SUSPENSE
RIVETING INSPIRATIONAL ROMANCE

YES! Please send me 2 FREE Love Inspired® Suspense novels and my 2 FREE mystery gifts (gifts are worth about $10). After receiving them, if I don't wish to receive any more books, I can return the shipping statement marked "cancel." If I don't cancel, I will receive 4 brand-new novels every month and be billed just $4.99 per book in the U.S. or $5.49 per book in Canada. That's a savings of at least 17% off the cover price. It's quite a bargain! Shipping and handling is just 50¢ per book in the U.S. and 75¢ per book in Canada.* I understand that accepting the 2 free books and gifts places me under no obligation to buy anything. I can always return a shipment and cancel at any time. Even if I never buy another book, the two free books and gifts are mine to keep forever.

123/323 IDN GH5Z

Name _____ (PLEASE PRINT) _____

Address _____ Apt. # _____

City _____ State/Prov. _____ Zip/Postal Code _____

Signature (if under 18, a parent or guardian must sign)

Mail to the **Reader Service:**
IN U.S.A.: P.O. Box 1867, Buffalo, NY 14240-1867
IN CANADA: P.O. Box 609, Fort Erie, Ontario L2A 5X3

Are you a current subscriber to Love Inspired® Suspense books and want to receive the larger-print edition?
Call 1-800-873-8635 or visit www.ReaderService.com.

* Terms and prices subject to change without notice. Prices do not include applicable taxes. Sales tax applicable in N.Y. Canadian residents will be charged applicable taxes. Offer not valid in Quebec. This offer is limited to one order per household. Not valid for current subscribers to Love Inspired Suspense books. All orders subject to credit approval. Credit or debit balances in a customer's account(s) may be offset by any other outstanding balance owed by or to the customer. Please allow 4 to 6 weeks for delivery. Offer available while quantities last.

Your Privacy—The Reader Service is committed to protecting your privacy. Our Privacy Policy is available online at www.ReaderService.com or upon request from the Reader Service.
We make a portion of our mailing list available to reputable third parties that offer products we believe may interest you. If you prefer that we not exchange your name with third parties, or if you wish to clarify or modify your communication preferences, please visit us at www.ReaderService.com/consumerschoice or write to us at Reader Service Preference Service, P.O. Box 9062, Buffalo, NY 14240-9062. Include your complete name and address.

LIS15

SPECIAL EXCERPT FROM

Love Inspired.
SUSPENSE

*With a dirty cop out to silence them forever, strangers
Leah Hampton and Jon Wilson must depend on each
other to survive.*

Read on for a sneak preview of
NO ONE TO TRUST
by *Melody Carlson.*

Leah Hampton felt her stomach knot as she watched the
uniformed officer in her rearview mirror. His plump
face appeared flushed and slightly irritated in the late
afternoon sun. Glancing around the deserted dune area,
as if worried someone else was around, he adjusted his
dark glasses and sauntered up to her old Subaru. She'd
noticed the unmarked car several miles back but hadn't
been concerned. She hadn't been speeding on this
isolated stretch of beach road—her car's worn shocks
couldn't take it.

Getting out of her car, she adjusted her running tank and
smoothed her running shorts, forcing an optimistic smile.
"Hello," she said in a friendly tone. "I was just heading
out for a beach run. Is something wrong, Officer?"

"Is that your car?"

"Yep." She nodded at her old beater. "And I know I
wasn't speeding."

"No…" He slowly glanced over his shoulder again.
What was he looking for? "You weren't speeding."

"So what's up?" She looked around, too. "Is there

some kind of danger out here? I mean, I do get a little concerned about jogging alone this time of day, especially down here where there's no phone connectivity. But I love this part of the beach, and I'm training for the Portland marathon and it's hard to get my running time in."

"You'll need to come with me," he said abruptly.

"Come with you?" She stared into the lenses of his dark sunglasses, trying to see the eyes behind them, but only the double image of her own puzzled face reflected back at her. "Why?"

"Because I have a warrant for your arrest."

"But you haven't even checked my ID. You don't know who I am." She held up her wallet, but before she could remove her driver's license, he smacked her hand, sending the wallet spilling to the ground.

"Doesn't matter who you are," he growled, "not where you're going."

Don't miss
NO ONE TO TRUST by Melody Carlson,
available March 2016 wherever
Love Inspired® Suspense books and ebooks are sold.

www.LoveInspired.com

Turn your love of reading into rewards you'll love with

Harlequin My Rewards

**Join for FREE today at
www.HarlequinMyRewards.com**

Earn **FREE BOOKS** of your choice.

Experience **EXCLUSIVE OFFERS** and contests.

Enjoy **BOOK RECOMMENDATIONS**
selected just for you.

PLUS! Sign up now
and get **500** points
right away!

Earn
FREE
REWARDS
HarlequinMyRewards.com
Join
Today!

MYR16R